THE VICIOUS CASE OF THE

VIRAL VACCINE

For further information, contact:
Tumblehome Learning, Inc.
201 Newton Street
Weston, MA 02493, USA
http://www.tumblehomelearning.com

Library of Congress Control Number: 2013936551

Noyce, Pendred
The Vicious Case of the Viral Vaccine / Pendred Noyce. - 1st ed

ISBN 978-0-9850008-7-5
1. Children - Fiction 2. Science Fiction 3. Mystery

Illustrations: Sun Cheng Yung (孫承雍)
Cover art: Sun Cheng Yung (孫承雍)
Cover design: mighty media®

Printed in Taiwan

10 9 8 7 6 5 4 3 2 1

THE VICIOUS CASE OF THE

VIRAL VACCINE

By Pendred Noyce and Roberta Baxter

Illustrated by Sun Cheng Yung

Tumblehome Learning, Inc.

TABLE OF CONTENTS

Chapter 1

The Universal Flu Vaccine

"That vaccine could make people really sick," Clinton burst out.

Mae clutched her current events report and looked out at the class. "It won't. My mother worked on this vaccine, and it's safe. Only crazy people think it isn't."

"Now, everyone settle down," Ms. Timilty, the long-term substitute teacher, said as she tapped on the desk. "Let Mae finish her report."

Clinton Chang leaned back with his arms crossed behind his head and glared at Mae. She continued her report.

"The CDC, that's the Centers for Disease Control, wants everyone to get the new shot that protects against all kinds of flu. It's called the Universal Flu Vaccine, and they'll start giving it out next week at pharmacies and doctors' offices around the city. The CDC is recommending that everyone get the shot because last year a record number of people died from the flu—50,000 in the United States. The scientists think that this flu season will be just as bad, but the shot will keep you from getting the flu not just this year but from now on. My mother is a research nurse and she helped with the clinical trials and no one got sick from it." Mae quickly walked back to her desk and sat down.

"But I heard that vaccines can give people the flu or even make them autistic," Sally Hingston said.

Mae whirled around so quickly that her braids whipped her cheek. She stared at Sally, her best friend, but then Clinton spoke up again.

"Some people get asthma so bad from the shots that they have to go to the hospital."

Mae frowned at him and started to say something, but Ms. Timilty interrupted. "Mae Jemison Harris and Clinton Chang! Stop this argument at once so others can present their reports."

Clinton slumped down in his chair and stuck his iPod ear buds back in his ears. Back to the slacker student that Mae had always known. She thought he might have changed some after their adventure solving the mystery of the stolen diamond chip. But apparently not—he was still the number one goof-off. And she still wanted to be the best student in the class.

She hardly listened to the other students' reports. She was still steaming about the comments from Clinton and Sally about the vaccine.

Finally, Ms. Timilty dismissed the class, and Mae walked home without talking to anyone. Her mother was still at work, but Mae let herself into the upstairs apartment. If she needed anything, Mrs. Peach, who had moved in downstairs when Professor Gufov left, would be all too ready to be helpful and nosy.

Usually Mae started her homework right after grabbing a snack, but today she was still so mad about how kids had reacted to her report that she flopped down on the couch and started flipping through TV channels. As she passed one channel, a building caught her eye and she pushed the remote to go back. A newscaster stood outside the county health building. Mae sat up and watched as the cameras showed what looked like a hundred people waving signs and yelling. The signs read, "Vaccines = Brain Killers" and "You'll Never Stick Me." One sign just showed a vial with blood dripping out of it.

The roar of the crowd grew louder as a woman in high heels and a bright pink suit stepped to the microphone. Mae could barely hear the announcer as he reported that Margo Smearon, candidate for U.S. Senate, was about to speak.

Margo Smearon tapped the microphone. "The government wants everyone to get this vaccine, but you have a right not to contaminate your body! Vaccines weaken the immune system. It's your right decide what's best for you, and this vaccine is not good for anybody. Do you want to lose your memory, be paralyzed, or get the flu? Do you want your child to become autistic?"

The crowd shouted, "No!"

"They call it the Universal Flu Vaccine, UFV," Ms. Smearon continued. "I call it a UFO, Unsafe Flu Object. No one knows what it might do to us."

The candidate kept talking and waving her arms, and the crowd applauded. So many people opposed to something meant to be good for them! With a sick feeling in her stomach, Mae turned off the television.

As she pulled books out of her backpack to start her homework, a key grated in the lock. It was too early for her mother to have finished work, and Mrs. Peach usually knocked. When her mother stepped through the door,

THE VICIOUS CASE OF THE VIRAL VACCINE

Mae's heart skipped a beat. Blood covered the front of her mother's gray shirt and the side of her face.

"Mom, what happened?" Mae ran to hug her and lead her toward the couch. "Are you all right? Did you have a car wreck?"

Her mother patted Mae's hair and made a soothing, clucking sound. "Don't worry, sweetie. It's fake blood, like people use for Halloween. Someone threw it on me as I left the research facility." She held Mae at arm's length. "I came home to change clothes and ask Mrs. Peach to fix you supper tonight."

"But why would anyone throw blood on you?" Mae asked.

"It was one of the vaccine protestors," her mother said. "The word got out that our facility did some of the clinical testing."

"That's awful," Mae said. "You're trying to help people, not hurt them. Don't they understand the vaccine will keep them from getting the flu?" Mae squeezed her hands. The sight of her mother covered in blood made her stomach hurt.

"Everyone is just getting really stirred up with irrational fears. Remember how we've talked about pseudoscience? People go with their feelings."

"You mean they hate vaccines because getting a shot hurts?"

Mae's mother shook her head. "It's more complicated than that. Someone tells them about a person who got sick after a shot and they don't stop to think about other possible explanations. They don't remember other people who got sick that same day without the flu shot. They jump on an idea and twist their observations to match their beliefs. If the facts don't line up with what they think, they look for new facts."

"So how do you convince them?"

"I wish I knew." Mae's mother walked into the bedroom and emerged with a clean face and blouse. "Listen, Mae, I've got to get to a meeting, so I'll send Mrs. Peach up to fix you spaghetti."

"She puts weird vegetables in it," Mae said. "Let me fix my own spaghetti, please?"

Her mother smiled. "All right, my independent child."

"And Mom, be careful."

* * *

As Mae spun the last bite of spaghetti onto her fork, a whooshing noise sounded behind her, and she turned in her chair to see Selectra Volt standing in a model's pose. "Greetings, Mae," Selectra said. "I hope the twenty-first century has been treating you zwiffily." She wore the same skin-tight outfit with pink puffballs and green boots as on her last visit. For the first time, Mae wondered if it was a uniform. Selectra's pink and green hair stood out in spikes, her green eyes glittered, and her bright pink nose shone.

"As a recruit to the Galactic Academy of Science, you know that I must verify your identity. Mae Jemison Harris, African-American, named for astronaut Mae Jemison. You have successfully completed one mission for the GAS."

"Wow, it's good to see you, Selectra," Mae said. "Where in the future did you come from this time?"

"Scoldings, Mae. You know this dudette can't tell you that," Selectra said, unhooking a device that looked like a smartphone from her belt. "Now, we need to get the other member of your team. Call Clinton Chang, Asian American, named for a president, and ask him to report immediately."

"Not Clinton, please," Mae objected. "He's not on my team, and I don't want him anywhere near me."

"Stop blintzing around, Mae. Not coolsome. As a member of the GAS you have a new mission and Clinton is part of the team. I won't spout another nano until he arrives."

"He has no concept of the integrity of science," Mae blurted. "He'll believe anything—true or not."

"You fear he's fallen under the influence of rumor and pseudoscience," Selectra said. "But this mission requires two GAS members." She sat daintily on the couch. "Do we have to request another team?"

Mae stared at her, frowning. Then she grabbed the phone, adjusted her glasses, took a breath, and called Clinton.

When Clinton answered, he said, "I hope you're calling to apologize, Mae."

"It wouldn't be zwiffy to hang up on me," Mae said quickly, hoping he would catch the clue. "My guest said I should ask you to come over right away."

"Oh." Mae could almost hear the thoughts skating around in that cluttered brain of his. "I'll be there."

When Mae opened the door to let Clinton enter, she didn't even look at him, and he pushed right past her.

"Do we have a new mission, personal dudette?" he asked, as he dropped his skateboard and backpack by the window.

"A plasma hot mission—much more difficult than the last. It requires teamwork and respectful discussion. Are you up to it?" Selectra gave each of them a hard look.

"We had an argument over the Universal Flu Vaccine," Mae said with a sigh.

"Yeah, Selectra. You're from the future. Is that vaccine safe?" Clinton asked.

"You know I can't tell you anything about the future, Clinton," Selectra said. "That's Rule Number Three. Remember the rules:

1: Verify recruits' identities on arrival.

2: Recruiter may not accompany recruits into the deeper past. I can't do the work for you.

3: I can't tell you anything about the future.

Clinton said, "But we're not still recruits, are we? We joined the Galactic Academy of Science after we found that diamond chip."

"Still recruits," Selectra said, "and still have to follow those rules to carry out your mission of 'Defending Scientific Integrity through the Centuries.' We need you to once more follow your duty to history and integrity. In fact, this mission is about the flu vaccine. Isn't that roasting?"

"But the UFV doesn't need us," Mae said. "It's already been tested and they'll start giving the shots next week."

"You two have been arguing over it, and so has most of the country," Selectra said. "This controversy must not be groobed up. You will travel back in time to learn how vaccines were discovered, how they work, and whether or not they are safe. Then your duty will be to tell others the scientific truth."

"Wow!" said Clinton. "You want us to expose how dangerous they are."

Mae stamped her foot. "They're not! They save lives."

"If you just stand there arguing, the mission will fail," Selectra said. "You already have fixed ideas, and that's what will make this mission challenging. My strongest advice to you is to keep your minds open. Can you do it?"

Glaring sideways at each other, Mae and Clinton nodded.

Selectra held out the smart phone-like device she had been holding. "Here's your Expedition Personal Assistant. Yep, we've decided to call it the X-PA. Like the name?"

Before Mae could respond, Clinton leaned forward and grabbed the Assistant. He turned away, but Mae leaned over far enough to see the X-PA over his shoulder. One red button said **Do Not Touch Until Ready to Travel**. A sideways 8 read **Loop** and another was marked **Candidates**

for Interview. Clinton pushed the **Candidates** button and a list showed up, starting in India, with other listings for England, Australia, the United States and China. Mae tried to read the list, but Clinton jiggled the X-PA too much for her to see clearly.

Selectra lectured in an official-sounding voice. "Remember to push the **Loop** button and wave the Assistant around everything you want to take with you. Keep arms and legs tucked in so you don't leave them behind. Remember the translation button, which will allow you to communicate with the candidates. Keep a close watch on the **Site Energy** bar. If it runs out, you'll be stuck wherever you are."

"We'll learn about vaccines in all these places?" Mae asked.

"Sure as roasting," Selectra said. "But don't reveal anything about the future to the people you visit. Just behave yourselves and ask your questions, and they'll forget about you in a few days."

Then Selectra inserted her fingers into a small bag attached to her belt. "These are for you so you won't be infected by any germs."

She handed Mae and Clinton each a small piece of transparent shiny cloth.

"What is it?" Clinton asked.

13

"It's a breather to protect you. Once you have it on, it's invisible, so no one will know you're wearing it."

"Awesome," Clinton exclaimed as he stretched the breather across his mouth.

Mae took her breather and was fingering its cool mesh when Clinton said, "Ready, Mae?" He held his finger over the **Loop** button.

"Not really," Mae muttered, but she inched closer to him so he could wave the Assistant around them both without Mae losing a foot or something. The X-PA screen showed the two of them like a 3-D drag and drop, and then the blackness closed in. Mae didn't even know which candidate Clinton had chosen for the first visit.

Chapter 2

Ground-Up Smallpox

India, 700 BCE

Mae opened her eyes and found herself gripping Clinton's arm. She dropped it fast and said, "Clinton, don't just carry us off without even consulting me!"

Clinton shrugged and gestured as if offering Mae all the land that lay before her. Rocky, bare hills surrounded them. A small song of water tinkled nearby, and a collection of huts made of mud and sticks littered the hillside.

"Where are we and when?" Mae asked.

Clinton looked at the Expedition Personal Assistant in his hand. "We're supposed to look for a guy named Nehal, and we're in India around 700 BCE. That's like 2700 years ago. How cool is that?"

"What would anyone in ancient India know about vaccines?" Mae wondered.

"Not sure," Clinton answered. "But you better put that breather on."

Mae stretched the breather across her mouth and nose. It stuck so lightly to her face she could barely feel it, and looking at Clinton she couldn't tell he was wearing one. "I wonder what these are made of," she said. "I hope we get to keep them when the mission's over. No more colds."

Clinton said, "Hey, Mae, behind you, some people are coming. Quick, what language do they speak in India? How will I know what translation to choose?" He sounded shaky. Mae turned to see five or six men marched toward them, carrying spears.

Mae tugged the X-PA out of Clinton's hand. She scrolled through the possibilities—Australian English, French, and Russian—all too modern. She scrolled faster. The men paused about ten feet away and pointed their spears at Clinton, who babbled in English.

"Hello, there. We're here to see this Nehal guy," he said rapidly in a trembling voice.

"Nehal," the man in front said, and then "wek-kasoddakka…"

Mae pushed the Sanskrit button, and the translation kicked in. "…Need the healer? Are you sick?"

"Just a little sick," Mae said. "We do need to see the healer."

"Do not get close to us," the man said, holding her off with both hands. He turned back toward the village, while the other men stood aside.

As Mae and Clinton walked into the village with the men escorting them, people emerged from doorways along the dirt path. Some of the adult villagers bore deep, round scars on their faces and bodies. Other adults and children lay on blankets, gazing up at them with dull eyes. Sores covered sick people's bodies, big spots that looked like pus-oozing boils. Flies buzzed around them. Mae pushed the breather closer against her face as Clinton shrank against her.

"Looks like we landed in Plague City," he said in her ear.

Their guide approached a house in the middle of the village. In the yard in front, an elderly woman stirred a large pot over a fire. The guide spoke to the old woman, but Mae couldn't catch the words.

Clinton grabbed the X-PA out of Mae's hand and, holding it in front of him like a shield, said, "We're looking for Nehal."

The woman turned to look at them. In among the wrinkles of her brown face, scars pitted her skin, and her white hair was so thin that her scalp also showed round scars. As the woman's large dark eyes examined them, Clinton repeated that he was looking for Nehal.

"You have found Nehal," the woman said. "Do you require healing?" She shuffled close and took hold of Clinton's arm. She pushed up his sleeve and examined his arm. Next she grabbed hold of Mae and did the same thing. She clucked and shook her head. "You do not appear ill, either one of you."

"No, we're not sick," Clinton said, just as he started coughing. He moved out of the path of the steam from the pot bubbling on the fire. A pungent smell rose from the pot, and Mae's eyes watered.

Nehal motioned for them to follow her into the hut. A small fire burned in the center of the darkened room, and bunches of dried plants hung from every part of the ceiling—healing herbs, Mae assumed.

Nehal took hold of Mae's arm again and ran her fingers over the skin. "You are very dark," Nehal said. "Are you sick from the sun fainting disease?"

Mae yanked her arm out of Nehal's hands and said, "No, this is my normal skin."

"What are these circles that cover your eyes?" Nehal said.

"Those are glasses so I can see. Don't touch them," Mae said, stepping back.

Clinton stepped forward and said to Nehal, "What's wrong with the people we saw? The ones with big sores?"

"Do you not know the pox disease in your village? Where do you come from?"

"We can't tell you anything about that. We just want to know how you treat such an awful sickness," Mae said.

"Maybe the goddess does not punish your village, but we are blessed to have her punishments and her healings."

Clinton looked at Mae and shrugged.

"Do you have a cure for this illness?" Mae asked.

Nehal's eyes held Mae's for what seemed like a long moment and then she said, "Once the disease takes hold, we offer mostly prayers. Many die. But maybe we can save the ones who are not yet sick. Come and let me teach you."

"What do you think this disease is, Mae?" Clinton asked in a whisper as they followed Nehal out the door.

"Not sure, but I think it looks like smallpox. I saw a picture in one of Mom's books," Mae answered.

"Smallpox!" Clinton stopped walking and stood with his mouth hanging open. "I thought maybe chickenpox. Smallpox kills people."

"I know," Mae said a little shakily. "So these breathers had better be good."

They caught up with Nehal just as she entered one of the huts. Two people, a woman and a young boy, lay stretched out on the floor. The mother huddled under several blankets, shivering. The boy had thrown off all of his blankets and lay moaning softly.

Nehal pulled a sharp-looking knife and a wad of what looked like dried dandelions out of a bag at her waist. Clinton backed out of Nehal's way as she headed for the small fire at the center of the room. She dropped the plant wad into a ceramic bowl and added water from a nearby jug. As she stirred the concoction with the knife, she muttered words that sounded like a chant, too low and hurried for the X-PA translator to catch.

Nehal lifted the mother's head and gave her a sip of the mixture from the cup. As the woman drank, Nehal continued chanting. Then she spoke to the woman, "I must scrape your arms and legs for the medicine I need for the rest of the village." The woman nodded.

Smallpox (10,000 BCE - 1980 CE)

 Smallpox is a viral disease found only in humans. Evidence of smallpox has been found even in ancient Egyptian mummies. Around half of all people throughout history who got the disease died of it. Many others were left with deep scars. When European explorers reached America, they brought with them smallpox germs that wiped out millions of Native Americans. Even in the 20th century, smallpox caused over 300 million deaths worldwide.

Smallpox spreads when people breathe in the tiny viruses. About two weeks later they become sick with fever, muscle pain, headaches, and vomiting. Red spots appear inside the mouth. Blisters cover the skin. After two weeks, if the victim lives, the sores begin to dry up and scab over.

Starting in ancient India around 1000 B.C., healers began trying to prevent this terrible disease. Dried up smallpox scrapings were scratched into the skin or inhaled into the nose. Ancient Chinese healers used the same methods. Sometimes this approach led to a full case of smallpox and even death.

In 1796, William Jenner, a doctor in rural England, discovered that injecting a related virus called cowpox prevented smallpox. Later vaccines were made from still another virus, vaccinia. These shots prevented 95% of infections. Heroic vaccination campaigns over many decades finally led to the death of smallpox. The last case occurred in Somalia in 1977. Today, children are no longer vaccinated against smallpox. The smallpox virus itself survives only in secret labs.

Nehal used the knife to scrape the sores on the woman's arm. Clinton gasped and Mae's stomach turned as the knife grated against skin and scab. The sick woman groaned as pus and a trickle of blood ran into the bowl that Nehal held to catch the scrapings. After Nehal had scraped both arms, she pulled more dried plants from her bag and spread them over the woman's sores.

As Nehal turned to the sick boy, Clinton said, "I'm not sure I can watch any more of this. I'm going outside." He thrust the X-PA at Mae and headed for the door.

Mae knew how he felt. Her stomach churned and her head spun, but she gritted her teeth and adjusted her glasses. The boy yelled as Nehal scraped scabs from his arms into the bowl, and when Nehal let go of his arms, he fell back toward his mother.

"Will you give the cure to my daughters and my husband?" the woman asked in a weak voice. "They are in the house of my husband's mother."

"They will receive the cure after the sun has gone down," Nehal said. She held the back of her hand against the woman's forehead, checking her temperature just as Mae's mother did when Mae was sick. "Drink the rest of the medicine I made for you, and make sure your son does as well. I ask that your body return to the balance of the wind, fire and earth by the blessing of the goddess Sitala."

When Mae and Nehal came out of the hut, Clinton joined them and asked the healer, "Aren't you afraid you'll catch the sickness? It looks so terrible."

Nehal frowned and touched her face. "But you can see from my scars that I already had the disease, when I was a child. All the rest of my family died, but now I am protected for the remainder of this lifetime. Surely the people in your village know this. Sitala brings the pox disease only once to each person. For this reason we take the scrapes from one who has the pustules, dry them carefully, and then scratch them into the healthy body. But we must wait until nightfall so that Sitala will bless the cure."

"And then the people don't get sick?" Mae said.

"Oh, yes," Nehal said. "They get sick. They get a sore on their skin where we scratch them and many other sores around it. But they do not die. They invite Sitala and she visits them gently."

"Who is Sitala?" Clinton whispered to Mae.

"Not sure," she answered.

Once the sun had gone down, Mae and Clinton followed Nehal to a large hut in the middle of the village. Several people stood waiting. Nehal opened a clay jar that she had brought. She shook out some dried flakes into a bowl and, adding water, ground it into a paste. Then she dipped a sharp stick into the paste and summoned the first person, an adolescent boy, to stand beside her. She grabbed hold of his arm, and he bit his lip and looked away. As Nehal slashed the point of the stick across his forearm, the boy's eyes flew wide open, but he kept silent.

One by one the people stepped forward to receive the treatment, from stoical women to children screaming and squirming in their parents' arms. Nehal chanted words so quietly that Mae and Clinton didn't know what she said.

Mae got close enough to peer into the cloth. The fragments looked like dried blood. "Oh, gross," she said to Clinton. "I think it's dried scabs."

"That's worse than gross," Clinton agreed. "We should really get out of here."

Nehal turned from her last patient and said, "Now for you two. I still have enough material left to treat two strangers from another village."

"Uh, no thank you," Mae said, stumbling backward. Beside her, Clinton gestured wildly for them both to leave. "We, uh, don't want to use up all your medicine."

Nehal shook her fingers in warning. "The goddess Sitala helps only those who have the courage to welcome her," she said. "Flee her and she will pursue you. She will seek

you out and find you, and then the pox disease will leap on you like wild dogs, and all around you will sicken and fall."

"I hope not," Mae stammered. "We have different ways. But thanks for showing us."

As the villagers stared after them, Mae and Clinton hurried away along the road. As soon as they had traveled beyond the reach of the firelight, Clinton stopped and held out his hand. "Man, I'm sure glad we don't have small-pox in the twenty-first century. I can't get out of here fast enough. So hand over the X-PA. Which candidate shall we interview this time?"

"No way. I'm not giving you anything. Let's visit Louis Pasteur, France, July 1885. You know, the guy who invented pasteurizing milk. I think he did something about rabies too." Mae looped the Assistant, and a deeper darkness closed around them.

Chapter 3
Pasteur and the Terrible Risk
Paris, July 1885

Mae felt her body slow from the time travel, and she carefully opened her eyes. She and Clinton had landed in a bare hallway. She tiptoed over to a tiny window and peeked in at a laboratory that looked a lot like where her mother worked, with lab benches and sinks cluttered with glassware. As Clinton joined her at the window, a voice behind them inquired, "Qu'est-ce qui se passe ici?"

Mae gulped and turned around to see a young man with a short beard and white coat holding a tray of bottles and what looked like syringes. Hastily, she scrolled down the Translator to find the French button.

28

The man continued to speak. "Qu'est-ce... going on here?"

"We're, we're," Clinton stuttered. Finally, he said, "We're students and we want to learn about Mr. Louis Pasteur's work."

The man peered at them. "You look too young to be journalists, so maybe you are in fact students," he muttered. Then more loudly: "I must ask the professor. Today is a critical day in our researches and we must work in peace."

"What's going on today?" Clinton asked. "Is it something about rabies?"

The man took a step backward, his face showing worry. "How do you know...?" The young man stopped speaking as an older man with brown hair and a short graying beard opened the laboratory door.

"Adrien, is it Madame Meister? Have you prepared the mixtures?"

"Yes, Professor, but I was speaking to these students. They want to know about your work."

"Are you Louis Pasteur?" Clinton asked before anyone else could speak.

"Indeed I am. Have you come to learn about germs and microbes? You must return another day. We must have solitude today for our researches." He took the tray from Adrien and backed through the laboratory door.

Mae stepped forward and caught the door. "Professor Pasteur, I'm sorry to disturb you, but we are only here for today and we have so wanted a chance to learn from you."

Pasteur turned to gaze at her, and then he said, "There is a short time until our subject arrives. Perhaps a brief lesson will be possible."

The next thing that Mae and Clinton knew, they were inside the laboratory, following Pasteur as he strolled among the tables covered in scientific equipment and glassware. Mae recognized some of it as the same as in her mother's lab. Other pieces looked very strange.

"I have been studying tiny creatures, germs that float in the air," Pasteur said. "I have found them in wine, milk and butter, causing spoilage. If I destroy the germs by heat, the milk or wine stays good. Would you like to see the germs through my microscope?"

"You bet." Clinton hurried forward.

"This is a drop of wine. Tell me what you see."

Clinton bent over the microscope. "All I see is my eyelash. Wait. I see big oval things, and around them are long skinny sticks."

"Good, good," Pasteur said. "The oval shapes are the yeast to ferment the wine. The sticks are the microbes that spoil it."

As Mae took her turn at the microscope, Pasteur continued, "In milk and butter I found germs that look different from these, but that also cause spoilage. I learned I could kill the germs and keep the milk good by heating it at mild temperatures. Then we found germs in animals with diseases like anthrax and chicken cholera."

"But even I, knowing how to find germs, was unable to save my precious..." Pasteur's words trailed off. He walked away to the window as Clinton and Mae looked on in surprise.

Adrien said quietly, "Two of the professor's daughters died of the typhoid. I not only work for him, he is my uncle. We all grieved with him on his loss. He feels driven to find a way to stop diseases, and that is our main work today."

"Please, Professor," Mae said. "How can we learn to fight these diseases in humans?"

Pasteur strode back across the laboratory. "I learned about a method called vaccination from the work of an Englishman, Edward Jenner. He found that injecting cowpox in a person stopped that person from getting smallpox."

"Smallpox?" Clinton asked. "That's what stopped smallpox? A shot of cowpox?"

"Yes," Pasteur said. "You see, cowpox is a weaker variant of the smallpox disease. Years ago, smallpox killed thousands of people every year. But Jenner discovered that milkmaids who got cowpox were immune to the smallpox. So he used the cowpox to prevent smallpox."

"Why don't we get smallpox vaccinations nowadays?" Clinton asked.

"Shhh." Mae poked Clinton with her elbow. "You aren't supposed to give away anything about the future."

Pasteur seemed to not hear them. He stared intently at the tray of vials and syringes that Adrien had carried into the lab. He said, "I have learned how to protect chickens from cholera and sheep from anthrax." He passed a hand over his forehead. "But today will be the hardest test of all."

Clinton turned to Adrien. "How do you prevent chicken and sheep diseases?"

Adrien said, "We have learned that disease organisms can be weakened and injected to prevent a disease. Cowpox works because it is a weaker disease, so the person doesn't get as sick, but it still protects against the smallpox." He took a breath. "We discovered by accident how to weaken microbes."

"By accident?" Mae asked. "That doesn't seem very scientific."

"We were studying cholera in chickens, injecting them with the cholera microbe. All the infected chickens died. Then the professor went on summer vacation, and one of the assistants accidentally left a vial of the cholera microbe sitting on the lab bench. When we came back, the professor injected a group of chickens with the left-out germs and none of them died. In fact, a week later, when we mixed a fresh batch of microbes, the fresh microbes didn't kill the injected chickens even though they killed new chickens just as well as before."

"Our mistake became a breakthrough," Pasteur said. Mae hadn't even realized that he was listening to Adrien's explanation. "We learned that we can weaken a microbe in air and inject it as a vaccine. It protects the animal against full-strength bacteria injected later."

"That's amazing," Clinton said. "But does the same thing work for people diseases?"

Before anyone could answer, a woman and a boy knocked at the door of the laboratory. Adrien opened the door. The boy, his legs covered in bandages, limped with difficulty, grimacing and holding onto his mother's arm.

"We are here, Monsieur Pasteur," the woman said.

"Good morning, Madame Meister," Pasteur greeted them. "How are you today, Joseph?"

The boy kept his gaze fixed on the floor. "The dog bites hurt, and I am frightened."

His mother said, "You must be brave, Joseph."

33

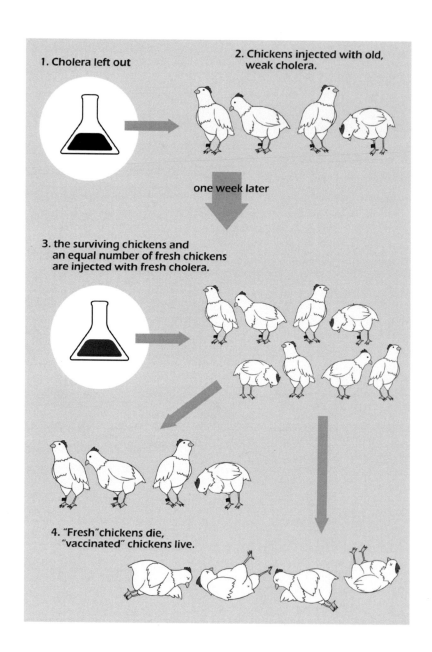

"What's going on?" Clinton asked.

Adrien answered quietly, "Young Joseph was bitten by a rabid dog a few days ago. Sometimes a person can be bitten and never develop symptoms of the disease. But if they do—well, you probably know that everyone who shows symptoms of rabies eventually dies. Once the disease takes hold, we can't stop it from killing. Joseph's mother heard of our researches into rabies and brought her son here. She begged Pasteur to heal her son. He told her it was too dangerous because we haven't done enough tests, but she reminded him that without his help the boy would most likely die."

The boy looked up at Mae, his brown eyes wide with appeal. Mae said, "You mean give him a vaccine to save his life? The professor will have to try."

Adrien shook his head. "I don't know. Professor Pasteur is not a medical doctor. If something goes wrong, the authorities could close down our laboratory and put an end to all our researches."

"Wait a minute," Clinton said. "I thought a vaccine had to be injected before you got the germ. If Joseph has already been bitten, maybe it's already too late."

Adrien said, "With rabies, sometimes the sickness takes months to arrive. We cannot give up so easily. Have you ever seen someone die from rabies? It is frightful. The patient endures high fevers and headache, then terrible pain, wild movements and a strange inability to swallow liquids. Eventually, after great suffering, he falls into a coma and dies." Adrien shuddered. "In the end, Pasteur asked the mother to come back today. He consulted with physicians to ask their advice about what was right and ethical to do. Even I do not know what he has decided." Adrien fell silent and leaned forward to catch Pasteur's words.

Pasteur spoke in a low voice. "You must understand the danger, Madame Meister. The injection I will be giving Joseph contains a weakened form of a substance that causes rabies. We have found that when injected in rabbits it protects against rabies, but we have never before tried it in humans."

Madame Meister said, "Please, Professor, do not tell me so much. Just save my son."

Pasteur sighed and gestured to Adrien, who handed him a tray with a small vial and a glass syringe. Pasteur drew a few drops of liquid from the vial into the syringe, and he said, "Joseph, I will give you ten injections, one each day. If you are brave, then after the shot, you may play with our rabbits."

Mae held her breath as the doctor injected the vaccine into Joseph's hip. The boy's face bunched up as if he was about to start crying. But as soon as Pasteur pulled the

THE VICIOUS CASE OF THE VIRAL VACCINE

needle out, the boy asked him, "May I play with the rabbits now?"

Pasteur led him to a room next to the laboratory. Through the open door, Mae saw rows of cages with rabbits and mice in them. She said in a low voice to Clinton, "I hate to think about them doing experiments on all these animals."

"Better than doing them on kids like Joseph," Clinton answered.

Mae thought about this, and then she asked Clinton, "What if your little sister got bitten by a rabid dog?"

Clinton rubbed his head. "I'd beg Pasteur to give her the vaccine. I'd promise to work in his lab washing glassware every day for a year if he'd just give her a chance."

Beside them, Adrien said in a quiet voice, "My aunt says that Pasteur barely slept the last few nights. He has been so worried about the safety of this set of injections for the child."

Pasteur returned to the lab and spoke again to Mae and Clinton, "We discovered that the rabies disease concentrates in the brain and spinal cord of the infected animals. So we had to find a way to weaken it so that it could be used for what I call a vaccine. As Jenner called his smallpox injection a "vaccine" from the word "*vacca*" for cow, so I call it. But how to weaken the rabies, that was the question. We cannot even see the microbe in the microscope! It hides, but then reveals itself in illness."

"Maybe it's a virus rather than a bacteria," Mae blurted out.

"Virus? What is a virus?" Pasteur asked in an eager voice.

"Now who's giving away the future?" Clinton said to Mae.

"Viruses are smaller than bacteria and can't be seen in a regular microscope," Mae said. To Clinton she added, "At least they won't remember what I said later, right? Selectra told us the memory fades."

As she spoke, Pasteur strode around the lab. "Could that be?" he said. "Too small to see?"

Then he returned to Clinton and Mae. "How do you know that? Are you conducting researches for yourselves? Are you spying on my work? Do you mean to expose me to the authorities?"

"Nothing like that," Clinton said quickly. "We come from the future, and we wanted to learn about your work on vaccines."

"The future?" Pasteur's eyes grew large, and he quit stroking his beard. "Are you two a vision of my worried,

Louis Pasteur (1822-1895) developed the germ theory and launched the science of microbiology. He invented the process of pasteurization and developed vaccines to prevent rabies in people and anthrax in animals.

Pasteur grew up in a poor French family. He showed a talent for drawing, so he received degrees in both science and art. Pasteur and his wife had five children, but only two of the children lived to adulthood because the others died of typhoid. Their deaths spurred Pasteur to study diseases. He showed that microbes grew in milk and wine and could be killed by a gentle heat, which became known as pasteurization. He also conducted studies on several animal diseases.

Pasteur knew of Edward Jenner's method of inoculating people with cowpox to prevent smallpox. He developed a weakened version of a chicken disease and called his discovery a vaccine, from the Latin word "vacca," meaning cow, in honor of Jenner's work.

His next project was a battle against rabies, a disease feared by all. The death rate of people who developed rabies was 100%. Pasteur extracted the virus from dried spinal cords of infected rabbits. The drying process weakened the virus, and injections made new animals immune to the disease. The true breakthrough came when the mother of Joseph Meister begged Pasteur to try it on her son. Joseph survived the treatment and Pasteur became famous for his rabies vaccine.

His germ theory led Pasteur to campaign for cleaner conditions in hospitals, which saved the lives of many people. In 1888, the Pasteur Institute for medical research opened in Paris, sponsored by donations from people around the world.

sleepless brain? But tell me, does rabies kill many people in your time?"

"I'm not sure about other countries," Clinton said. "In our time, I only know that dogs get rabies vaccines."

"So, dogs are vaccinated so they won't get the disease and bite people," Pasteur said. "Brilliant! Tell me more about your future world."

Mae said, with a poke of her elbow into Clinton's side, "We're not allowed to tell you more, Professor Pasteur. Please explain how you weakened the rabies."

"We use the dried up spinal cords from infected rabbits. We dry each spinal cord for a week or more in a special jar, and the drying process weakens the disease. Then we dilute the material from the dried spinal cords in more and more solution. We start the injections with the weakest solution and move to the strongest." Pasteur paused. "It works in dogs." Then in a low voice to himself, he said, "I am on the edge of mysteries and the veil is thinner. Pray God that the boy lives."

He shook himself and spoke again to Mae and Clinton, "You, children, do you study science?"

"Yes," Mae said. "I want to be an astronaut." She hesitated as she realized that Pasteur would have no idea what an astronaut did. "I want to fly between the planets. I like to study science."

"To fly through the night sky! Amazing. You must study hard and learn all you can," Pasteur said. "Chance favors the prepared mind. With no preparation, no successes."

He nodded at them and walked back to the room of animals where Joseph stood cradling a bunny in his arms. Mae took the opportunity to glance at the X-PA in her hand. The **Site Energy** bar hovered at ten percent.

"We better go, Clinton," Mae said. "Thank you so much, Professor."

"But what about Joseph?" Clinton asked as they walked back into the hall. "Will he live?"

"Maybe we can research it later at home," Mae said.

"We've learned about rabies and smallpox," Clinton said as they walked into the hallway, "but nothing about any of the shots we get at home. "What about measles or flu or mumps?"

"I was wondering about that," Mae answered. "I can't even remember what shots I've had, can you?"

"Not all of them," Clinton said. "Do you think we can travel back home and find out about that and what's going on?"

"You mean and then come back to the past again?" Mae asked, peering at the X-PA. "I don't know. But wait.

Look here." She pointed at a new button in among the **Candidates for Interview**. The button said, **Return to Base**. "Shall I try it?"

She drew a loop in the air around herself and Clinton, pressed the button, and felt the darkness close in as they left Pasteur's lab.

Chapter 4

Vaccine Controversy, Round Two

When Mae opened her eyes, she and Clinton stood on her new living room carpet. Her empty plate still sat on the coffee table, and someone was knocking on the door.

"Mae, is everything all right?" Mrs. Peach called through the door.

"Hide," Mae said to Clinton. She pushed him into a coat closet.

"I'm fine, Mrs. Peach. Thanks for checking," Mae said as she opened the door a few inches. "I'm going to be doing homework the rest of the evening."

"Are you sure? I mean, I don't want to be nosy, but I just saw those awful people on TV throwing things at the scientists and I wanted to be sure that you were all right."

"I'll call you if I need anything," Mae said, and Mrs. Peach nodded and headed back downstairs to her apartment.

Mae opened the closet door for Clinton and found him with his hand clamped over his mouth and laughing eyes above.

"I felt like a burglar," he said.

Mae laughed with him.

"Let's check the TV and see what's going on, or maybe the news on your computer or something," Clinton said.

As soon as Mae turned on the TV, they saw pictures of a large crowd. They couldn't hear what the people were yelling, but Mae stiffened, making her hands into fists. "What's happening now? That's the building where my mom works. I hope she's all right."

"That's her building?" Clinton said. "Did you read the crawler? More scientists had fake blood thrown on them, and some got threatening e-mails. This is getting serious, Mae."

Mae glared at him. "But you're on the crowd's side."

45

"Listen, Mae, I know your mom's not trying to hurt anyone. She's brave, like Nehal and Pasteur. That doesn't prove the vaccine is safe, but no one should threaten her or any of the others."

Mae nodded, biting her lip, and Clinton said, "Why don't you call her?"

Mae pulled out her cell phone. After dialing, she waited, pushing her glasses up farther onto her nose over and over again.

"Mom, are you all right? I saw the news on TV. I'm fine. Love you!" She lowered the phone.

"I had to leave a message," Mae said in a low voice. "She must still be in her meeting."

"I'm sure she's fine," Clinton said.

Taking a breath, Mae said, "Let's watch more of that news." She turned up the volume. Margo Smearon, candidate for U.S. Senate, stood once more in front of the crowd. Her speech sounded the same as her earlier rant, so instead of listening, Mae examined the crowd as the camera panned around. The people seemed to be taking in everything Smearon said, and some yelled and nodded their heads at her words. Others waved signs. Mae noticed one man with a sign that had the word AUTISM crossed out with a big red X. The man, young and chunky with shaggy brown hair, looked familiar, and Mae moved closer to the screen. How did she know him? Where had she seen him? Before she could find the answer, the camera moved on.

Another lady spoke at the microphone. "My son was perfectly normal until he got his MMR shot, and then he got autism and started having seizures." She looked like she was about to cry. "I don't want anyone else to have to suffer through that."

A man stood up and said, "My son got a really high fever after all the shots he got when he was two. He almost died. No one should be forced to get this Universal Flu Vaccine if they don't want it. In fact, no responsible parents should let their kids be injected."

Clinton shifted around on the couch and then burst out, "Mae, I've got to go home and see about my family. I'll meet you back here in an hour."

Before Mae could say anything, he was out the door.

After Clinton left, Mae watched more of the anti-vaccine rally. It bothered her that no one spoke up about scientific evidence. The stories about sick children were sad, but what if the sicknesses were not caused by the vaccines but just happened around the same time? Besides, what if those children had gotten the diseases instead? *You can't prove something scientifically by listening to stories*, she thought.

She turned off the TV, wandered around the apartment, touched the books in the bookcase, and looked in the cabinet for a snack until she decided she didn't want anything. Finally she walked into her mother's room. Then her phone beeped for a text message. Her heart beat a little faster when she saw that it was from her mother. The text read, "Fine, home soon. Business trip tomorrow. Mrs. Peach to stay with you."

Mae sent a text to Clinton: "Text when u r coming. Meet me outside."

When Mae entered her room, she found her books and notebook scattered across the bed. She picked up the notebook and began writing down what she and Clinton had learned about vaccines.

Smallpox: Nehal prevented bad cases by giving people a small case of smallpox. Jenner used cowpox, which is related but weaker.

Rabies: Pasteur weakened the microbe by drying and then vaccinated people after a rabid dog bit them.

She had never heard of anyone getting rabies or smallpox, or even a smallpox shot. Dogs and cats got rabies shots, but people didn't. Why not? And why was Clinton so worried about the UFV?

Just then a key turned in the lock. The door opened, and footsteps sounded softly on the carpet. Mae ran to the living room to hug her mother.

"Wow, that's quite a greeting, twice in one day," her mother said. "Is everything OK?"

"Oh, it's all zwif...I mean, fine," Mae said. "I was just thinking about all this vaccine stuff. Mom, do you have a list of the shots I've had?"

"Are you worried about the flu vaccine, Mae?"

"No, I just don't know what other shots I've gotten. Why don't we get smallpox vaccine anymore?"

"Smallpox! You don't have to worry about that. Now, I had a smallpox vaccination when I was young." Mae's mother pulled back her sleeve so Mae could see the patchy round scar on her arm. "But kids nowadays don't need that one anymore. Smallpox has been eradicated, wiped out. You see, smallpox can only be transmitted from one person to another, so once enough people were vaccinated, the virus had no place to go and the disease was beaten for good."

"What vaccines do we get now?" Mae asked.

"I have a list of your vaccinations on the computer. You can look at it while I pack. Tomorrow I have to go to the state capital for more meetings." Mom sighed. "I wish I could just be back in my lab, but that's how it goes."

Mae stood behind her mother as she logged on to her computer account. She pulled up a spreadsheet titled, "Mae's Vaccination Record."

Wow, Mae thought as she scanned the list. *I got a lot of shots as a baby.* The list showed weird abbreviations like DTaP, MMR, IPV, and something called varicella. Mae typed those symbols into a search engine and came up with explanations. DTaP was for diseases called diphtheria, tetanus, and pertussis, whatever those were. MMR she remembered as being for mumps and something. The computer showed it as for mumps, measles, and rubella. She read that rubella was also called German measles. It wasn't a bad illness in most people, but if a pregnant lady got rubella, her baby could be born blind and deaf. *That's cool*, thought Mae. *I got the rubella shot so I couldn't make a pregnant lady sick. My shot protected little babies who weren't even born yet.*

The IPV, she read, was a shot to prevent polio, but before she could read more about that disease, her phone beeped with a text. "Waiting outside, ready 4 time trip."

Mae found her mother in front of an open suitcase, folding a skirt. Mae said, "I'm going off to bed pretty soon." She hoped that didn't count as a lie. She would be going to bed soon by the clock. It was just she had a lot of investigating to do first. "Will you be here in the morning?"

Her mother closed a suitcase full of clothes and kissed her. "Good night, sweetie. I'll leave before you wake up."

Mae closed the door to her room and quietly tiptoed out of the house.

"My family is all OK," Clinton said. "But I found out that my dad scheduled us for the UFV first thing Monday. We need to find out if it's safe."

"Why are you so worried about it, Clinton?" Mae asked.

Clinton looked down, scuffed his toe around in the grass, and said in a voice way too quiet for him, "My sister Chelsea almost died after the flu shot last year." He lifted his head and glared at Mae. "As soon as we got our flu shots, her asthma started really bad. She could barely breathe, so we rushed off to the ER."

"But then she was OK?" Mae asked.

"She had to stay in the hospital for two days," Clinton said.

"How do you know it was the shot that made Chelsea sick?" Mae asked.

"What else would have caused it?" Clinton demanded. "I mean, I don't have proof, but Chelsea got the shot and then she got sick. And what if it happens again?"

Maybe he's right, Mae thought. *I mean, this happened to a family I know.* All at once, it seemed much harder not to believe that a personal story proved a scientific fact. She said, "It must be rough for her to have asthma."

"Yeah," Clinton said. "It's really scary. Let's go wherever we need to get this figured out."

"Where are we headed next?" Mae asked.

Clinton held out the X-PA and scanned through the list as Mae looked over his shoulder.

"Let's go there," he said as he pointed at Jonas Salk, Ann Arbor, Michigan, April 12, 1955.

Chapter 5

Dr. Salk and the Iron Lung
Michigan, 1955

Mae felt the familiar swoop in her stomach as the X-PA pulled her into another time. When her vision cleared, she stood on a street lined with trees. Nearby, a sign read, "University of Michigan." Down the street, a crowd of people stood near the doors of a large building.

"What's this about?" Mae asked. "What's happening?"

Clinton held up the X-PA. "I don't know. It's 1955. Who's Jonas Salk?"

A car drove past, and Clinton swiveled his head to watch it. "Wow, look at that old car! My dad would love this."

"We're not here to look at cars," Mae said. "Let's find out what's going on."

As they walked toward the crowd of people, a woman in a dark dress and pearls held out a can. She said, "A dime for the fight against polio?"

A label on the can read, "March of Dimes."

"Excuse me," Clinton said. "Can you tell us why this crowd is here?"

"You mean you don't know?" The woman raised her eyebrows. "It might be the end of polio forever." She lowered the can. "In that building over there, Rackham Hall,

scientists are meeting to hear whether Dr. Salk's vaccine works. We should get the news very soon."

"Polio," Clinton said. "I think I got that vaccine."

"Then you must be a Polio Pioneer," the lady said. "Thank you for your service."

"I'm not a pioneer," Clinton said. "In the future, everyone gets vaccines."

"Careful, Clinton," Mae said.

Clinton ignored her as usual and went on, "We came here from the future to learn more about how vaccines started."

"The future?" the lady asked with a frown. "Do you have a fever, young man? Do you have polio now?" She took a step backward.

"No," Mae stepped in. "We are students trying to learn about Dr. Salk, and we don't understand exactly what's going on. Why is this such a big deal?"

"Haven't your parents told you why they don't let you go swimming?" the lady said. "It's as frightening as the atom bomb. In 1952, more than 59,000 American children got polio. Many were paralyzed and some died." Her voice sounded as if she might cry.

She dug into her purse and pulled out a black and white photo. "This is my daughter, Margaret. Because of polio, she has to live in an iron lung."

Mae and Clinton looked at the picture and into the eyes of a girl about their own age. They could see only her head as she lay on a bed with the rest of her body inside what looked like a huge metal can.

"Why is she lying inside that thing?" Mae asked.

The lady frowned and said, "Are you making fun of me? The polio paralyzed her chest muscles, so she has to stay in the iron lung to breathe."

"Forever?" Clinton asked in a horrified voice.

Before the lady could respond, a large crowd of people surged around them, and Mae grabbed Clinton's arm so they wouldn't get swept apart. The lady disappeared in the crowd.

"Forever?" Clinton asked again, this time looking at Mae.

"I don't know," Mae answered. "It's hard to think about."

A teenage boy stood next to them at the curb of the street. He leaned on crutches, and a gleam of metal glinted at the bottom of his leg. Mae pulled Clinton over and asked the boy, "Did you have polio?"

The boy looked at her as if she was from outer space and then said, "Of course. Look at my leg. I had polio about four years ago."

"Can you tell us what happened?" Clinton asked.

"My mother said not to go out, not to go swimming, but it was hot and all my friends were going. So I snuck out of the house and went down to the swimming hole. A week later, I came down with a fever, and then that afternoon, I couldn't move my legs."

"Because of polio?" Clinton asked. "It comes from swimming?"

"People say it does. I don't think the scientists know for sure." The boy shrugged. "Hey, my name is Robert. I don't really mind your questions, by the way. A lot of people see my leg brace and look away as if I'm just pitiful. But even a president can have polio, you know."

Mae introduced herself and Clinton. Then she asked, "What happened when you were sick?"

"I couldn't move my arms and legs, so the doctor sent me to a special hospital with a slew of other polio victims. I was lucky because it never spread to my chest, so I could still breathe. I stayed there for five months and my arms got better. But my legs don't work well anymore, so I have to wear these braces and use crutches." He pulled up his pant leg and Clinton and Mae could see that metal bars ran up the sides of his leg, tied together with leather straps.

"I hope Dr. Salk really has beaten this thing. Then no one else will have to use these." Robert tapped a fingernail against his braces.

"We're going to try to talk to Dr. Salk," Mae said, pulling Clinton away. "It was nice meeting you, Robert."

"Excuse me, sir," she said to a tall man with a pencil stuck behind his ear. "Can you get us a chance to talk to Dr. Salk?"

"You and most of Michigan," the man said. "Everyone wants to talk to him today."

"We're students," Mae went on. "We've been studying all about vaccines. Smallpox, rabies…Now we want to learn about his polio vaccine."

The man looked down at them. "Students, are you? I suppose it's possible he'll talk to you. Have you had the polio vaccine yet?"

Clinton said, "Sure, we've both had it."

"Follow me," the man said. "I'll see if Jonas can give you a couple of minutes. I'm John Troan, reporter for the Pittsburgh Press. I came to hear the announcement about the polio vaccine. Jonas Salk is a friend of mine, and this is the big day."

"Can you tell us about it?" Mae said.

"Last year, field trials of Salk's vaccine started. You know what it was like if you've had the vaccine. Kids and mothers lined up for blocks. I reported on those early trials. So far, 1.8 million children have taken part. Jonas and I have talked about it many times when we meet for lunch. Today, he'll finally learn if the vaccine was effective."

Jonas Salk (1914-1995) developed a polio vaccine given to millions of children. At the time, polio was more frightening to parents than any other disease, because it seemed to come from nowhere, bringing death or paralysis to its victims.

Salk was born in New York City. His parents valued education and encouraged their son to attend college. He wasn't especially interested in science as a child, but in college he excelled and decided to attend medical school to become a researcher.

During his last year in medical school, Salk worked for Dr. Thomas Francis in New York City in a research program on viruses. When Salk finished his internship, no one would hire him because he was Jewish. Dr. Francis had moved to the University of Michigan, and he hired Salk to work on developing an influenza vaccine for the military, which was successful.

Salk wanted to direct his own research lab, and the University of Pittsburgh gave him that chance. The National Foundation for Infantile Paralysis asked him to help in research against polio. Through the March of Dimes, thousands of volunteers helped raise money for his work.

Salk planned to make a killed virus vaccine. Other scientists, including Dr. Albert Sabin, believed that only a live virus would provide enough protection. Salk developed and tested his vaccine amid the controversy. He even vaccinated his own sons. To ensure the testing results were valid, Dr. Francis conducted double-blind test with 1.8 million children. Before the results were announced on April 12, 1955 even Salk did not know if his vaccine would work.

The announcement that the vaccine was safe and effective brought relief to parents everywhere. Salk decided not to take out a patent on his vaccine. He wanted his vaccine to be affordable to people everywhere.

"You mean he doesn't even know if it works and he gave it to a million kids anyway?" Clinton asked.

"It's a scientific trial," Troan said. "It's the only way to find out for sure if a treatment works. See, the kids were randomly assigned. Four hundred thousand kids got injected with the vaccine. Two hundred thousand got a placebo, which means an inactive injection, a shot with no vaccine. And another 1.2 million were in the control group that got no injection at all. So now we get to find out how many kids got polio in the different groups. Only Dr. Francis knows who got the real vaccine, who didn't, and what the tests say. Now he's about to announce the results. I'll let you in on a secret. I heard from one of my sources they're already getting ready to release the vaccine for everyone. So I'm pretty sure today's announcement is going to be good news."

Mae and Clinton pushed through the crowd to stay close to Mr. Troan. Clinton said in a low voice, "It would be a drag to be one of the kids who got the fake vaccine. A shot that does nothing, who would want that?"

"Hey," said Mae. "I thought you were the one who was against vaccines."

"This is different. This isn't the flu. I'd hate to end up in one of those iron lungs, that's all."

When Mr. Troan reached the building, he showed a police officer a card with "Press" on it and said, "These two kids are with me."

Mae and Clinton followed the journalist up the stairs. As they climbed, Troan said, "It's a historic day for another reason. It was ten years today that President Franklin Delano Roosevelt died. He had polio, you know."

"Really?" Clinton said. "He was paralyzed?"

"Yep, paralyzed legs. Spent most of his time in a wheelchair, though he didn't want people to know," Troan said.

When they reached the third floor, they entered a large room full of desks and telephones. Men in white shirts and ties stood around everywhere talking and writing on pads of paper. Many of them greeted Troan as he led Mae and Clinton to a desk and phone in one corner. Mae couldn't help but feel a fluttering of excitement in her stomach. One way or another, this was clearly a day that mattered to millions of people.

Troan leaned against a wall. "While we wait for the speeches, I should tell you that Jonas has had a rough time," he said. "When he finished medical school, some people wouldn't even hire him because he's a Jew. And then when the first vaccine, not the one Jonas made, but another one, was first tested, some of the children got polio."

"You mean they got polio from the vaccine." Clinton's voice squeaked, and Mae could imagine him thinking that the same might happen to his sister.

"Yeah, so they stopped that vaccine. They made some mistakes, but Jonas will do better." Troan stood up straight. "Oh, wait, this must be the press release from Dr. Francis."

Newspapermen swarmed toward the door and reached over one another to grab purple sheets of paper from a man who was passing them out.

"It works!" one of them yelled. The journalists rushed to the phones and shouted into them, "The Salk vaccine works!" Mae heard one man say, "Polio is defeated!"

Troan yelled into a phone like everyone else. "Polio is conquered!" he began, and he dictated a newspaper story. Once he had finished, he said, "Well, my report is done. Kids, we might be able to meet Jonas later. Want to give it a try?"

"Sure," Clinton said. Mae and Clinton followed Troan downstairs to a crowded auditorium. They squeezed into the back and stood against the wall. The man at the podium talked and talked, but the chatter around the kids drowned out most of what he was saying. After what seemed like a long time, the man introduced Jonas Salk of the University of Pittsburgh Virus Lab.

As soon as the audience heard the name, they stood up from their chairs, clapping and whistling. A tall man with dark hair and glasses walked slowly across the stage. When he reached the podium, the audience settled down and he began to speak.

He mentioned many names, thanking people Mae knew nothing about. She wished he would explain about the vaccine.

When his speech was over, Troan leaned down. "Let's get a hot dog and then go try to talk to Jonas. I know where he and his family are staying."

After they fought their way out of the crowd, Troan led them to a sidewalk food cart where a sign read: "Hot dogs 25% off in honor of mankind's conquest of polio." After they finished their hot dogs and Clinton tried to rub a splotch of ketchup from his shirt, Troan led them down a series of streets. Finally he stopped in front of a modest house. A kite flew in the sky above the backyard, and a pair of boys ran around the side of the house, laughing. "Salk's sons," Troan said.

When he knocked on the door, a police officer answered and let him in. Dr. Salk came to greet them. "Great day, Jonas," Troan said, shaking his hand. "I brought two students who want to learn about vaccines."

"Well, tell me what you know," Salk said as he sat down in the living room.

Mae and Clinton slowly sank into the couch and Clinton said, "Uh... uh... we know a little about what it's like when people get sick with polio. And we know that vaccination is when you give people a little bit of a germ to prevent them from getting sick with the real disease."

"What do you know about bacteria and viruses?" Salk said.

Mae could answer that one. "Bacteria are bigger than viruses, but both cause disease."

"Right. Viruses are not actually living organisms. They are little packets of protein and DNA that invade cells. They take over the cell's machinery to reproduce and spread through the body, causing disease. Polio is a virus, and there are three strains or types. The vaccine that was announced today will prevent most polio infections of all three kinds."

"How did you make the vaccine?" Mae asked.

"It took a while. Seven years ago, the National Foundation for Infantile Paralysis asked me to study polio and see if a vaccine could be made. It's taken us all this time to do it."

"Infan what?" Clinton said.

"Infantile paralysis," Salk said. "It's another name for poliomyelitis, or polio as most people call it. The Foundation has a program called the March of Dimes. Volunteers collect dimes from the public to finance our research. Surely you've heard of it."

"There was a lady collecting dimes outside the research building," Mae said.

"Ladies like her have collected dimes from a hundred million people to help beat polio," Salk said.

"A hundred million," Mae repeated, feeling guilty that she had no money in her pocket to chip in. She said again, "But how did you find the vaccine?"

Dr. Salk tugged on his ear. "First we spent years injecting monkeys to sort out the different types of polio. Finally, a team of scientists at Harvard learned how to grow poliovirus in the lab, and that made it easier. We grew lots of virus, killed it with formaldehyde and mixed the three types together. When we injected the killed virus into monkeys, their immune systems responded. We could take blood samples and see that antibodies had developed. Do you know what antibodies are?"

"Not really," Clinton said. "My mom just talks about little soldiers that protect our bodies. Are those antibodies?"

Mae hugged herself, thinking of those poor monkeys always getting injections and having their blood drawn.

"That's pretty close," Salk said. "Whenever bacteria or viruses enter your body, white blood cells called lymphocytes start to make antibodies, which are specially shaped molecules that fit onto parts of the germ like jigsaw pieces. You see, every virus or bacteria has its own set of molecules on its surface. These surface molecules are called antigens. Antibodies recognize a surface antigen and attach to it until it can be killed by the white blood cells."

"I get it," said Clinton. "The antibodies are like sheriff's deputies, and they're carrying around a picture of a bad guy, and when they recognize the bad guy they jump on him and hold him down until the sheriff arrives."

Salk laughed. "Yeah, that's pretty much it. Now, it takes a while, like a week or two, for the lymphocytes to make enough antibodies to handle all the germs. Sometimes by that time the infection has already done a lot of harm. So we make vaccines to give the body a head start. By giving people a germ that's dead or very weak, we stimulate the body to make the antibodies without giving the person a bad disease. Once people have been vaccinated, the lymphocytes remember what that antigen looks like and how to manufacture antibodies. If they ever see that antigen again, the lymphocyte factories pour out antibodies double quick because they already have the blueprint, and the virus or bacteria is destroyed before it can do any harm."

"Hmm," Mae said. "So that's why people only get diseases like chickenpox once—because their bodies learn how to fight it off." She thought for a minute. "But then why do we have to get flu shots every year? And why do we keep getting colds over and over again?"

Salk looked startled. "Flu shots? Who's giving you flu shots? I started my career working on an influenza vaccine for the military, but I didn't know anyone was giving it to kids."

"Uh," said Mae, as Clinton elbowed her. "I was just imagining how it might be in the future."

"Well, widespread vaccination against the flu would be a huge advance, of course. You may not know this, but in 1918, a flu virus swept around the world in what we call a pandemic— even worse than an epidemic, because it af-

fects many countries—and it killed around a hundred million people, most of them healthy young adults."

Clinton stood with his mouth open, and then moved his lips silently. *A hundred million people!*

"But you see, the problem with influenza is that we think the strain changes every year. If the new strain has its own antigens, that's like a bad guy getting plastic surgery so your sheriff's deputies can't recognize him to arrest him. We'd have to make a new flu shot every year." He shook his head.

"Unless..." said Mae, thinking aloud. "Unless you could somehow find something about him that didn't change, like his ears or his liver or something." She looked in excitement at Clinton. "And then you could make a Universal Flu Vaccine, and you could inject everybody just once."

Salk laughed again. "That's visionary, all right. Who knows, maybe you'll be the one to discover that." He leaned back in his seat. "The big disagreement when I started working on polio was whether the vaccine should use killed virus or just a weakened virus. Either would stimulate an antibody response, but I believed that a killed virus would be safer. Then we had to learn how to make it and how to manufacture enough doses for millions of children. Our testing worked with monkeys, but it would have to be tested on people. Safety has to come first."

Dr. Salk stood up and began walking around the room. "When I worked with influenza, we found out that sometimes the vaccine left the bloodstream too fast for enough antibodies to form. So we had to use a carrier to help keep the vaccine antigens around. A carrier that helps antibodies form is called an adjuvant. We generally use mineral oil."

"You put oil in the shots?" Clinton said with a grimace.

"Yes, for two reasons," Salk said, holding up his fingers. "First, the thicker liquid stays in the body longer and allows it to make more antibodies. Second, the oil irritates the immune system so that it really goes into high gear to get rid of the intruders. We found that an adjuvant was needed for the polio vaccine."

"So, you and Dr. Francis decided to do a test and see if the vaccine worked," Troan said.

"Yes," Salk said. "It had to be done right, in a scientific manner. Francis set it up so that some children received our vaccine and others received a placebo, and neither knew which they got. Then they measured how many children developed polio." Salk paused, and then he looked at Troan and smiled. "It works, John. It works."

Just then a woman entered the room. "Jonas, they want you to be on television tonight, on the See It Now show."

"Do they?" Salk said, and he turned to the children. "Excuse me, I must take this call."

Troan stood. "This is a great day," he said. "The Salk vaccine will keep thousands of children from getting polio. But we'd better be going."

As they left, Clinton pulled the X-PA out of his pocket and looked at it. He showed Mae with his thumb and finger that not much time was left. They followed Troan down the street. Outside a barbershop, a man was painting "Thank you, Dr. Salk!" on the front window. Other people still stood around talking excitedly.

"It looks like the whole town is celebrating," Clinton said.

"More like the whole world," Troan answered. "But I've got to leave you two and get back to work. It's been great to meet you. I'm always going to remember that bit about the sheriff's deputies and the plastic surgery."

"Thanks, Mr. Troan," Clinton said.

Mae and Clinton walked away from the street of shops and excited people. Once they found a quiet neighborhood, Mae took the X-PA from Clinton and said, "Where next?"

Clinton bent over the device. "Cool, here's one in Australia. Let's go there. Kangaroos, here we come!"

Chapter 6

Macfarlane Burnet and the Cloned Avengers

Melbourne, 1959

When Mae opened her eyes, she saw a tall building that looked like an apartment building.

"So this is Australia," Clinton said, sounding disappointed. "I don't see any kangaroos."

"Where are we?" Mae asked.

Clinton looked at the X-PA. "It says we're in Melbourne, and this is the Walter and Eliza Hall Institute of Medical Research in 1959. We're supposed to interview some guy named Macfarlane Burnet."

Clinton led the way to the front of the building and Mae followed. She wasn't sure how they would find Burnet, but adjusting her glasses and taking a deep breath, she walked up to a desk. A man stood there collecting his mail, but Clinton stepped around him and spoke to the receptionist.

"We're here to speak to Dr. Macfarlane Burnet," Clinton said.

The receptionist frowned, but the man collecting mail spoke up. "You're looking for Mac? Do you have an appointment?"

Mae said, "Not exactly. We're here to learn about vaccines and antibodies and all that." She held out her hand. "I'm Mae, and this is Clinton."

The man shook hands with both of them. "Gustav Nossal, pleased to meet you. Let's see if the boss has time for a couple of scruffy students. He's rather shy, you know, and always busy. But you've certainly come to the right place to learn about immunology. Follow, please."

As they walked down the hall, Clinton said, "Immunology?"

"The study of how the body protects itself against disease." Dr. Nossal led them into a sparkling, white lab and Mae relaxed. She felt as if she was visiting her mother's workplace.

"You don't sound like an Australian," Clinton said to Dr. Nossal.

THE VICIOUS CASE OF THE VIRAL VACCINE

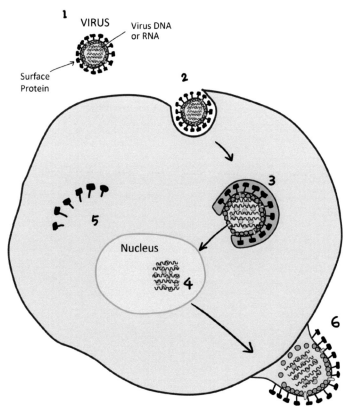

1. Virus has proteins and genetic material -- DNA or RNA

2. Virus enters cell

3. Virus is carried to nucleus

4. Cell copies virus DNA or RNA and uses it to make proteins

5. Some virus proteins cause cell injury

6. New virus copies bud off of cell and go to infect other cells

Dr. Nossal laughed. "You're right," he said. "I was born in Austria and my family moved to Australia to escape Hitler when I was 8 years old. You don't sound Australian either. Are you not Americans?"

"Yes, we're students learning about viruses and vaccines," Mae said.

"I first wanted to be a virologist, one who studies viruses. Do you know how viruses work?"

"We just know they're small and vicious," Clinton said.

"Viruses are not living organisms. They don't have all the molecules and mechanisms to produce life, so they have to live off other organisms. They are little packets of protein filled with genetic instructions, either DNA or RNA, but not both. Cells must have both to make proteins and reproduce. So viruses invade a cell, maybe one in your nose or throat or stomach, and they hijack the cell's mechanisms. The virus releases its DNA or RNA and uses the cell's own factories to make copies of itself. Eventually the cell is so full of viruses it bursts, letting the copy viruses go out to infect other cells."

"Leaving a trail of blown-up cells behind them," Clinton said.

"Precisely. Viruses are destroyers of cells. The word 'virus' even comes from a word meaning poison," Dr. Nossal said.

"They're poison to me," Clinton agreed. "I hate getting sick."

Dr. Nossal said, "Now that you have a little background, let's see if we can find Dr. Burnet, who is my mentor and Australia's greatest researcher." He led them to a white door, knocked, and pushed it open. "Dr. Burnet? Some students to see you. They want to learn about vaccines and immunology."

Mae and Clinton followed Dr. Nossal into Dr. Burnet's office. Dr. Burnet laid down his pen and rose to greet them. The doctor was about sixty years old, broad-shouldered, with a square jaw and iron gray hair.

"Come on, now, Gus," Dr. Burnet said. "You know I'm supposed to be working on my book. I don't have time for interruptions."

Clinton stepped forward. "Is your book about immunology, sir? If you can explain your work to two kids like us, think how clearly you'll explain it to your readers."

"You make a good point." Burnet perched on the corner of his desk. "Tell me what you know about antibodies."

Clinton bounced in place. "Sure. See, antibodies are like sheriff's deputies carrying around a picture of a bad guy, and—"

Dr. Burnet's forehead wrinkled, and Mae broke in, trying furiously to remember what Dr. Salk had told them.

"Antibodies are molecules made by special blood cells called lymphocytes. They fit like puzzle pieces onto markers called antigens on the surface of bacteria and viruses."

"Yeah, I was just getting to that," Clinton said. "The antibody deputies snap the handcuffs on the bad guy antigens, and then the big cells come around to arrest them."

"To eat them, actually." Dr. Burnet laughed. "I can see how the two of you together might make one very good student. But tell them our problem, Gus."

Dr. Nossal nodded and picked up a piece of chalk. "Here's the puzzling thing. How can the body make an antibody to every kind of bacteria and virus that exists in the world? There are so many, more than you can imagine."

Mae thought for a minute. "Maybe a lot of germs have the same surface markers, I mean antigens. Or close enough, like cowpox and smallpox, so the same antibodies can attack both of them."

Nossal raised his eyebrows. "Very good answer! But in fact we know that's not usually the case. Think of the colds you get several times a year. A slightly different virus, and you're not immune to it at all."

"Well," suggested Clinton, "maybe the antigen thingy kind of teaches the blood cell how to make antibodies that fit just right. Maybe the antigen gets stuck on the lymphocyte cell and makes a dent on its surface, and then the cell oozes out this protein to coat it, and then the cell learns how to make the coat just like a coat factory, and then…" He waved his hands in the air, talking fast.

Dr. Burnet laughed again, and Dr. Nossal raised both hands. "Hold on, there, young man, slow down. In fact, something like your theory was very popular in the forties. The idea was that the antigen somehow taught any lymphocyte cell it hit to make the right antibodies for that antigen. But then, you see, every cell should be able to make every kind of antibody, and it turns out that's just not true."

"Oh," said Clinton, looking dejected. "I guess I'd be a failure as an immunologist."

Burnet stood and addressed him. "Not at all. You came up with a good, testable idea. In science, finding out when an idea doesn't work is very important. For one thing, it makes you go back and think harder, and that's always fun. Tell them the next idea, Gus."

Nossal nodded. "Right. The main idea is that when an infective agent, like a virus or a bacteria, enters the body, it floats around in the blood until it runs into a molecule that matches it. The matching molecule attaches to it, and then, just as we said, cells from the immune system come and eat it up. Niels Jerne proposed that there are millions of different kinds of molecules of antibodies in the body, so when

CLONAL SELECTION OF LYMPHOCYTES

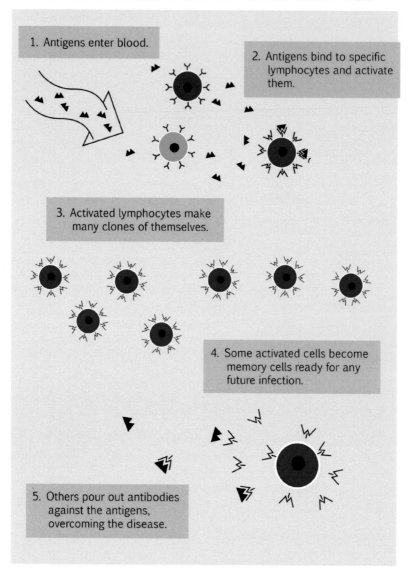

1. Antigens enter blood.

2. Antigens bind to specific lymphocytes and activate them.

3. Activated lymphocytes make many clones of themselves.

4. Some activated cells become memory cells ready for any future infection.

5. Others pour out antibodies against the antigens, overcoming the disease.

an infective agent, or antigen, enters, there will be always be an antibody to find it."

"Millions?" Mae asked.

"Really, what Jerne said is that there about 10^{17} antibody molecules in the body. That's a one and 17 zeros."

"That's, like, gazillions," Clinton said. "How could those all fit?"

"You have to remember that molecules, even large proteins, are tiny compared to cells," Dr. Nossal said. "And still, even all those antibodies don't provide enough protection against a disease. Once the clump of antigen and antibody attach to a lymphocyte cell, the cell begins to multiply. It clones itself and makes millions more lymphocyte cells identical to itself. That army of cloned cells is what finally overcomes the disease antigen and helps the body fight off infection."

"Cool," Clinton said. "Clone wars."

Burnet spoke up. "My underlying idea is that each antigen-antibody pair stimulates production of two cloned lymphocytes. One fights the infection by dividing many times and pouring out antibodies, while the other lasts longer and becomes a memory cell that remembers the antigen. We call this the clonal selection theory. It's not a random process, but one that is very selective."

Mae thought for a minute. "How can you find out if this idea is true?"

Nossal said, "At first, I thought my boss's proposal of the clonal selection theory was way off. But I didn't tell him. I just kept working and thinking about it. Finally, I dreamed up an experiment to see if a single cell makes many antibodies or only one."

"So what did you find out?" Mae asked.

"I thought each lymphocyte would produce two or three different antibodies. But my experiments proved that hypothesis to be false. Each lymphocyte produced only one antibody type. My work proved that Mac was right about the clonal selection theory. I published a paper about my research." He turned to Clinton. "So you see, young man, being wrong can be very important to progress in science, at least if you keep an open mind and look at the evidence."

"How do vaccines fit in?" Clinton asked. "If we already have antibodies, why do we need vaccines?"

"I think I know the answer," Mae said. "Vaccines are like an early warning system. They make it so the lymphocytes clone themselves and get ready to fight a disease without the person having to get the disease the first time."

"Exactly," Nossal said. "A few antibodies are not enough to keep us from getting sick. It takes a week or two for the body to make enough antibody to fight off a new disease. That's why you're usually sick for about a week when you get a cold. For some serious diseases like smallpox or polio, a week might be too long. A vaccine forces your body to make lots of antibodies and also memory lymphocytes, giving your body a rapid response team to be ready if you ever run into the real germ. And the more we learn about how the immune system works, the better we'll get at making vaccines."

Mae glanced at the X-PA and got a jolt. The **Site Energy** bar was short and bright red. Mae yanked on Clinton's sleeve and said, "Thanks for talking to us, Dr. Nossal and Dr. Burnet. We better go now and let you get back to work."

"It's great to meet young people who are interested in such things. Keep learning," Dr. Nossal said. But Dr. Burnet just lowered his head, picked up his pen, and returned to his writing, as if they had never come.

Mae and Clinton left the Institute and found a quiet corner in the back of the building.

"Where do we go next?" Clinton asked. "It was cool to find out about how the body makes antibodies for self-defense, but need to find out more about man-made vaccines and whether they're really safe."

"This looks like the next one," Mae said.

Mae pushed the candidate listing that said, "Maurice Hilleman, New Jersey, 1963" and drew a loop around herself and Clinton with the X-PA.

Sir Frank Macfarlane Burnet (1899-1985) was an Australian virologist and founder of the field of immunology.

"Mac" Burnet was a shy and studious boy. He received his doctor of medicine degree in Australia in 1924. He then went to London, where he studied the bacteriophage virus. He earned his PhD in 1928.

After marrying, Burnet returned to Australia, where he worked at the Walter and Eliza Hall Institute. There he discovered the bacteria causing psittacosis, caught from parrots, and Q fever. In fact, Burnet caught Q fever in the lab. He may have felt better when the bacterium that sickened him was named Coxiella burnetii after him.

During World War II, Burnet worked on two diseases common among soldiers, scrub typhus and influenza. Unfortunately, his flu vaccine, tested on 20,000 soldiers, did not work.

After the war, Burnet turned his attention to immunology. He studied graft-versus-host disease, where a transplanted organ attacks the person who has received the transplant. He also studied immune tolerance and developed his clonal selection theory. Burnet's younger colleague Gustav Nossal showed that each B-lymphocyte produces only one antibody. This finding supported the clonal selection theory.

For his research, Burnet received many honors and medals, including a knighthood. He received the Nobel Prize for his work on immune tolerance. This research explained how the immune system distinguishes between its own proteins and those that come from outside the body. Burnet himself, though, considered the clonal selection theory to be his most important contribution to science.

Chapter 7

Maurice Hilleman and the Cotton Swab

New Jersey, 1963

Clinton and Mae landed on the carpet in what looked like the darkened hallway of a private house. As Mae tried to get her bearings, Clinton moved down the hall and looked in one of the doors. "Hello," he said.

Mae joined him as a voice asked, "Who are you? Did Daddy send you?"

A little girl lay in bed in a darkened room with the blankets pulled up to her chin. The sky visible through the window glowed faintly in the moonlight.

"We're Clinton and Mae," Clinton said, and he looked at Mae for help.

The girl, who looked about five years old, groaned and shifted in the bed. She said, "Daddy says I have the mumps. You better go so you won't get sick."

"We've been vaccinated for mumps, right Mae?" Clinton asked.

"Yes. It's part of the MMR shot, the one for mumps, measles and rubella." Mae walked closer to the bed and said, "Can you tell us your name?"

"I'm Jeryl Lynn Hilleman," the little girl said. "My neck and head hurt." She settled back on her pillow and let out a groan.

Right under the girl's jaw, her neck was swollen, and the flush on her cheeks suggested a fever. Clinton gazed down at her with a look of concern. Probably thinking about his sister, Mae thought.

Just then footsteps sounded in the hall. Clinton beckoned frantically to Mae, and they both jumped into a closet across the room from Jeryl Lynn's bed. Clinton pulled the door almost shut, but they could still see out the crack. A man came into the room and touched Jeryl Lynn on the head.

"Some kids were here, Daddy," Jeryl Lynn said.

"Oh, sweetie, it must be your fever giving you visions." The man went into the bathroom and returned with a damp cloth, which he used to wipe his daughter's forehead. Then he laid down the cloth and said, "I'm sorry, Jeryl Lynn, but I need to get a sample from your throat. It will help with Daddy's work."

"Will it hurt?" Jeryl Lynn asked.

"It might for just a minute, but then it will be over."

He opened a package and pulled out a cotton swab. As he carefully inserted the swab in Jeryl Lynn's mouth, Mae felt her throat close up. She'd had her throat tested enough times when she had strep. Jeryl Lynn whimpered, and Mae almost felt herself gag.

The man stuck the swab into a tube of yellow liquid, twisted down the lid, and stuck it in his pocket. Jeryl Lynn turned onto her side and snuggled into her pillow, and her father rubbed her back until her breathing grew slow and steady. Then he slipped out of the room and down the hall.

"We'd better follow him if we can," Clinton said, and they tiptoed out of the closet.

Mae's heart thudded in her throat. If they were caught in someone's house, they'd get in big trouble. What would the Galactic Academy of Science do if two recruits got themselves arrested sometime in the past?

In the hall, Mae and Clinton heard voices coming from another room. Clinton led the way through the living room and quietly opened the front door. A car sat in the driveway.

"We could get in the car," Clinton said. "That's probably how he's leaving."

"How do you know he's going anywhere now?" Mae asked. "It's the middle of the night."

"I don't know for sure. I mean, I suppose he could store it overnight in the fridge, but I don't think he would have taken it in the middle of the night unless he meant to use it right away."

Impressed, Mae followed Clinton into the back seat of the car, and they scrunched down onto the floor, taking up as little space as possible. Clinton was right. As soon as they settled in place, the front door of the house opened and closed.

Mae held her breath as Jeryl Lynn's father got in the car and started the engine. Clinton's shoe poked into her shoulder, but she didn't dare move. The car backed up, turned, and went forward. The man drove for what seemed like an eternity and then made a few quick turns and stopped.

Clinton and Mae waited for several minutes after the driver left, and then they lifted their heads, stretched, and climbed out of the car. The car stood in front of what looked like an industrial building, and Jeryl Lynn's father was going in the front door. A large sign near the road read "Merck & Co."

"Uh, maybe we shouldn't go after him right now," Clinton said. "Like you said, it's the middle of the night."

So they hid behind a clump of bushes and waited. Nothing happened.

"What now?" Mae demanded. "This is the stupidest visit ever. Does the X-PA expect us just to wait until morning?"

Clinton shrugged. "Any better idea?" He looked at the X-PA. "We've got plenty of time. Maybe it doesn't burn through Site Energy as fast when we're doing something really boring."

"Like sleeping," Mae said, and she scooted around to try and get comfortable. Clinton stretched out on the ground, looking up at the sky. Neither of them said anything for a while. Then Clinton asked, "Mae, your mom works on vaccines. How does she know they're safe?"

"We haven't really talked about it," Mae said. "She showed me my vaccine record and boy, I got a lot of shots, so she must think they're OK. She does believe that everything should be tested scientifically and people shouldn't just go by their feelings."

"I've been thinking about the people we've met. I mean, who would ever think about not getting the polio shot? You could end up paralyzed and have to spend your life in one of those iron lungs," Clinton said.

"Yeah, that was pretty scary," Mae agreed.

"But the flu won't paralyze you or kill you, so why should everyone get that UFV?"

"I don't want to have the flu, and some people can get really sick from it," Mae said. "The TV said fifty thousand people died from the flu last year. I mean, if a person is old or weak or sick already, you could give them the flu, and then they could die because of you."

"Maybe," Clinton said, but Mae was pretty sure he wasn't convinced.

The next thing Mae knew, she heard voices coming from the parking lot. She must have dozed off. Clinton sprawled out next to her with his feet sticking out of the bush. She poked him, and he slowly drew in his legs and rubbed his eyes.

Then a man's voice said, "Hey, what are you kids doing here? Are you runaways? Should I be calling the police?"

Mae stood up and said, "We want to learn about vaccines, so we came to your building. We heard that your company makes all kinds of vaccines."

The man looked at Mae and Clinton with a skeptical stare and said, "It's awfully early. How long have you been here?"

"Never too early to learn," Clinton said.

Mae added, "And school starts at nine."

The man raised his eyebrows and nodded. "Your curiosity and eagerness are impressive. I might be able to give you a quick tour. Wait here and I'll see if I can get permission."

He walked to the front door of the building, where a uniformed guard now stood at the door. Mae heard part of the conversation. "Just kids…not likely to be spies trying to see the operation…"

Finally their discoverer came back to them. "I'm John, by the way. You really want to learn about vaccine manufacturing?"

"Oh, yes," Mae said.

They followed John into the building, and he walked straight down the main hall to the back door. Pointing out the glass door, he said, "It starts out there in the chicken houses."

"Chicken houses?" Clinton spoke as if he couldn't believe his ears.

"Dern tootin'. We need lots of chickens to lay lots of eggs. That's what we grow the vaccine in, actually in the unborn chicks inside the eggs. Right now we're working on a measles vaccine. "

Gross! Mae thought, but she kept her mouth shut. John led them around the corner into a long hall at the back of the building.

"We let the virus grow inside the eggs and then we transfer it to other eggs and so on. Each switch weakens the virus more, but it will still produce antibodies in the human body. Do you know about antibodies?"

"Sure, we learned about them from Dr. Salk and Dr. Burnet," Clinton said.

John stopped and stared at them as Mae gave Clinton a poke. "Salk and Burnet? Burnet in Australia? You two really get around."

Mae said quickly, "We used e-mail. Um, I mean regular mail, we used regular mail. We wrote letters." She shuffled uncomfortably, and then, as a distraction, she asked, "What do you do with the virus once it grows?"

"The next step is purification, to make sure the vaccine isn't contaminated. Then we have to mix it to the right strength."

They looked through a window into a gigantic room filled with large metal vats. Workers dressed in white clothes and masks stood throughout the room watching the equipment. Clinton started to push open the door next to the window, but John grabbed his arm.

"Sorry," he said. "You can't go in there. You might contaminate the vaccine or equipment, or you might catch the measles."

"I've already been vac—" Before Clinton could finish, Mae poked him again. But John wasn't listening. He was already walking ahead to the next window. This time they saw thousands of small glass bottles rattling down a conveyor belt.

"The bottles have been sterilized, and at the end over there, the vaccine is put into the bottles and sealed. Each bottle has several doses, and they'll be shipped to pharmacies and doctors' offices around the country."

"John, who is this?" Jeryl Lynn's father, with dark circles under his eyes and a scowl on his face, walked down the hall toward them.

"These young people want to learn about vaccines, so I'm giving them the quick tour. Mae and Clinton, this is Maurice Hilleman. He's the chief virologist for Merck and Company."

"Little tours are all very well, John, but I have another project for you to work on. I collected a specimen from Jeryl Lynn this morning." He frowned at Mae and Clinton, and for a moment Mae thought he was going to accuse them of breaking into his house and car. But he just said, "Jeryl Lynn has the mumps. I want to culture the virus so we can see about a mumps vaccine. Finish up your little tour and let's get to work. We're going to call this one the Jeryl Lynn strain." He turned away.

"Wait a minute, Dr. Hilleman," Clinton said.

Dr. Hilleman pivoted and stared down his nose at Clinton. "Well?"

"Eggs. You make the vaccines in chicken eggs. What if the person who gets the vaccine is allergic to chicken eggs?"

Maurice Hilleman (1919-2005) invented more than 30 vaccines. He also discovered many new viruses.

Just after Maurice Hilleman's birth on a Montana farm, his twin sister and his mother both died. Hilleman's father sent him to an uncle and aunt to raise him on a farm nearby. There he worked with chickens. Since many viruses are grown in chicken eggs, this experience proved useful to him later in life.

Hilleman's brother helped him attend Montana State University, where he won a graduate scholarship to the University of Chicago. For his PhD research, he studied chlamydia, which was thought to be a virus. Hilleman showed that instead it was a special kind of bacteria that grew only inside cells.

During World War II, Hilleman worked on the influenza virus and discovered how it mutates. This work led to the development of a flu vaccine that likely saved thousands of lives.

After the war, Hilleman began working at Merck & Co. In 1963, he cultured tissue from his daughter's throat when she had the mumps. He named the virus he isolated the Jeryl Lynn strain after his daughter, and he used it to develop a vaccine against mumps. Overall he developed or assisted in the creation of vaccines for encephalitis, mumps, measles, rubella, meningitis, hepatitis A, hepatitis B, chickenpox, and pneumonia.

Besides his work on vaccines, Hilleman helped discover the viruses that cause colds, hepatitis, and some forms of cancer. When Maurice Hilleman died, few people knew his name, but the vaccines he'd invented had saved or improved millions of lives.

Dr. Hilleman raised his eyebrows. "The processing should remove almost all chicken protein. However, we would advise anyone with an egg allergy to avoid the injection. An adverse reaction would of course be possible."

"An adverse reaction? You mean like an asthma attack?"

"It's not inconceivable." Dr. Hilleman walked down the hallway, leaving John, Mae and Clinton behind.

"Not very polite, is he?" Clinton said in a whisper to Mae.

"Er, I'll escort you out," John said.

Clinton asked him, "So if people are allergic to eggs and they can't get the vaccine, what happens? Just tough luck for them? You just let them get the disease?"

John sighed. "There are always some people who can't get a shot for medical reasons or who don't mount a good immune response even if they do get the shot. What we hope is that if enough people get immunized, the illness will never spread that far. We call that herd immunity."

Clinton said, "You mean like if you gave shots to enough cows in a herd, a cow disease couldn't spread to the last few cows that never got shots."

"Yep," said John. "The brave cows who get shots are helping to protect the weaker cows who can't get them. Now here we are." He opened the front door for them and shooed them out. "Off you go."

Mae turned to Clinton, "Is Chelsea allergic to eggs?"

"I don't know. I just started thinking about it. The thing is, sometimes on weekends after a big breakfast of bacon and eggs, she does start to wheeze."

They returned to their hiding place behind the bush and checked the X-PA. The two possibilities in front of them were **Return to Base** and **Candidate for Interview Andrew Wakefield, anti-vaccine crusader, England.**

"Oh, man, I think we better visit this one," Clinton said. "I mean, everyone else has been in favor of vaccines. We should learn about the other side. One more visit?"

Mae nodded, so Clinton looked around to be sure that no one was watching and then drew the loop around them. He pushed the button and darkness closed in.

Chapter 8

The Doctor and the Journalist

London, 1998 - 2010

"Where are we, Clinton?" Mae asked.

Clinton looked at the Personal Assistant and said, "We're in England, February 26, 1998. Supposed to learn something from Dr. Andrew Wakefield."

"I guess he must work here," Mae said, as she looked up at a building. A sign on the building said Royal Free Hospital School of Medicine.

A man in a raincoat walking by asked in an English accent, "What are you youngsters doing here?"

"Please, sir, we're students," Mae said politely. "Can you tell us what's happening here?"

"It's a press conference led by some doctor named Wakefield. He's published a research paper, and the journal invited the press to see a video about his work. Rather unusual procedure."

"Are you going in?" Clinton asked. "Can we please come along?"

"It's for a research project of our own," Mae added.

"I'll see if I can get you in. I'm Seldon Miller, writing for a newspaper up north."

Before long, Clinton and Mae stood in a large room with reporters packed around them. Up front stood a table with five men.

The video played, showing several minutes of Dr. Andrew Wakefield being interviewed about his research on autistic children. Many of these children, he said, had developed normally until they received the MMR vaccine. Soon after the shot, Dr. Wakefield said, the children stopped talking, lost some of their abilities and suffered severe gastrointestinal illness.

"Gastro what?" Clinton said in Mae's ear.

"I think it means stomach aches, diarrhea, stuff like that," Mae whispered back.

Dr. Wakefield went on to describe examinations he had performed on twelve children. He found inflammation of the colon and swollen lymph nodes. When the interviewer asked him if this was a result of the MMR, Wakefield

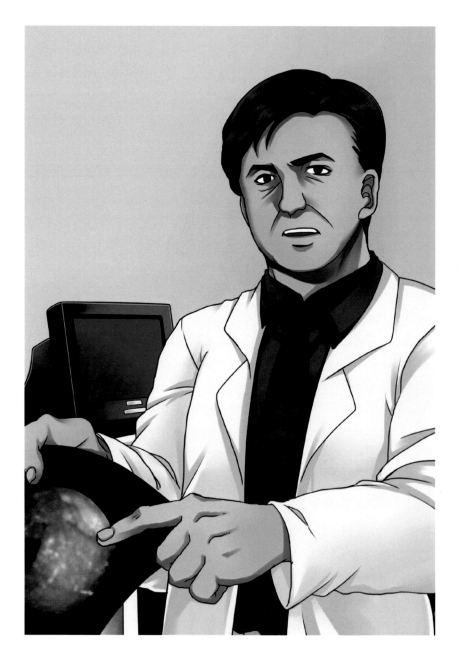

said it raised a question about the MMR vaccine. He suggested that the three vaccines for measles, mumps, and rubella should be given separately until more study was completed.

When the video stopped, the men at the front table introduced themselves, and one of them, a strong, healthy-looking man with square features, identified himself as Dr. Wakefield. One of his colleagues spoke about the need for more research and said that for now, children should continue to receive the MMR vaccine. Then Dr. Wakefield began to speak about how the vaccine, the gastrointestinal findings, and the symptoms of autism seemed to happen in the same children around the same time. Every reporter in the room leaned forward and began to scribble on a notepad.

Wakefield said, "I cannot support the continued use of the three vaccines together."

Clinton looked at Mae with his eyebrows raised. The noise level in the room went up as the reporters began yelling out questions. The men at the table waited, but the rowdiness continued. Finally, one man, who Mae thought was the head of the medical school, banged on the table, and the room calmed down. He said, "Millions of children have been vaccinated with the MMR vaccine, and countless lives have been saved from these diseases. If this study were to precipitate a scare that reduced the rate of immunization, children might start dying from measles."

Reporters scurried for the door. Seldon Miller turned to Clinton and Mae and said, "Will you be all right? I've got to get this to my paper."

"Sure," Clinton said.

After the crowd thinned out, Mae and Clinton went outside and walked to a quiet place at the back of the building.

"Do you think he's right, Mae?" Clinton said with a frown. "1998… You and I both got the MMR around that time. And my sister got it when she was a baby. What if she gets autism? That's what Jimmy Franks has, right?"

Mae thought of Jimmy. He came with an aide to their class at school, but he hardly talked to anyone and sometimes he hid under a chair in the corner and curled up in a ball. Their teacher just let him stay there, and sometimes he didn't come out all day.

"I think he has autism," Mae said. "But I'm sure Chelsea's safe, because she got the injection years ago, and she hasn't shown any symptoms, right?" She chewed on her lip. "It sure sounds bad. Those mothers said their kids' symptoms started a couple of weeks after the shot, when their kids were one or two years old. But is that proof? I wonder when autism usually starts. I wonder if some kids get autism even without shots. Who else can we interview to figure this out?"

Clinton showed her the X-PA, but the list of candidates for interview was blank. Although the **Site Energy** bar still stretched in green across the screen, the other buttons showed just empty space.

Clinton poked at the X-PA, saying, "What's going—"

Before he could finish his sentence, Mae felt the squeeze that meant they were traveling. But the swoop felt different—not as strong, more as if they were moving in slow motion. Clinton's eyes widened, and his mouth hung open in a scream.

When the darkness cleared, Mae found herself still planted in the same spot outside the hospital. But the sunlight streamed in from a different angle, and a cool breeze stirred her hair.

"What just happened?" Clinton said.

"I don't know," Mae said with a quaver in her voice. "What if the Assistant goes wacky and we can't get..." She couldn't even finish the sentence.

Clinton frowned and tapped on the face of the Assistant. The **Candidates for Interview** button was still blank.

"Maybe we should check where we are, or I mean, *when* we are," he said.

They crossed the street in front of the hospital. Atop a stack of newspapers locked inside a newsstand case, a headline caught Mae's attention.

"Hey, Clinton," she said. "Look at this."

One headline read "Measles Jab Turned My Son into an Autistic Child." Another one proclaimed, "I Want Justice for my James."

"So it's true." Clinton said. "How come we still get that shot?"

Before Mae could answer him, a voice behind them said, "Are you still working on that research?"

It was Seldon Miller.

"Mr. Miller, this is going to sound strange, but what day is today?" Clinton asked.

"Yes, that's strange, but it's a Tuesday, middle of March," Mr. Miller said.

"What year?" Mae asked.

Mr. Miller looked at her as if she had two heads. "Are you two all right? It's only about two weeks since I saw you at that crazy press conference—March 1998."

"What else has happened?" Clinton asked.

"Thirty-seven doctors just held a big meeting and said Wakefield's research was rubbish. Said his conclusions were worthless. But he keeps making headlines. Gotta go write up this story."

"Thanks, Mr. Miller," Clinton said, and he and Mae watched Mr. Miller hurry down the sidewalk.

"I don't know why the X-PA stuttered like that and sent us here," Mae said. "Now I'm even more confused about Dr. Wakefield and vaccines."

"Hey, look, Mae." Clinton held out the Assistant. "The candidate buttons are back."

Mae leaned over and looked.

"The candidate on top is Brian Deer, and he's here in London in 2004," she said. "Maybe it's more of this story."

"Try it," Clinton said. "Quick, before the X-PA acts up again."

They rounded the building again and Clinton looped the Assistant. As darkness closed in Mae felt her body jerk forward.

They landed on the sidewalk of a busy street. A building across the street was marked The Sunday Times.

"Do you think Brian Deer is in there?" Clinton wondered.

"Just have to ask, I guess," Mae said.

They entered the newspaper building and asked the woman at the front desk for Brian Deer.

"Do you have a news tip for him?" she inquired.

"We'd like to talk to him," Clinton said.

The woman picked up a phone, and in a few minutes, a man with a narrow face and close-cut brown hair strode in their direction.

"Brian Deer," he said, holding out his hand.

"We're Mae and Clinton," Clinton said. "Can you tell us anything about Dr. Andrew Wakefield?"

"Ah, you read my piece about his phony research?"

"You wrote about him? Could you tell us what you said?"

"What do you know?" Mr. Deer asked.

Mae counted off on her fingers. "We know that he says that the MMR vaccine causes autism and that makes kids act funny, and that it has something to do with a stomach bug or something, and that people got really upset..."

"You've got a lot of it. Autism is a developmental disease of the brain. It makes people not see the world the way the rest of us do. They seem to live in their own world and sometimes they won't talk or interact with other people. Wakefield claimed that the MMR vaccine caused children to get an inflammation in their digestive system which let the measles vaccine get to their brain and cause autism."

"That's awful," Clinton said.

"Ah, but is it true?" Mr. Deer said. "I spent hours researching his claims and found out some very troubling information. It turns out that before Wakefield even started his research project, he was paid a lot of money—five times his annual salary—by a lawyer preparing a lawsuit against vaccine companies. Wakefield and the lawyer decided to find kids whose symptoms of autism started soon after they got their MMR shot. So they sent out letters recruiting parents who already thought the vaccine caused problems for the kids. That's who they got in their study."

"Wait a minute," Mae said. "When do kids usually show signs of autism?"

"Usually between one and three years old."

Mae thought back to her vaccination records. "And they get their MMR shot around 15 to18 months, right?"

Brian Deer nodded.

"So doesn't that mean just by chance those two things—getting the shots and showing signs of sickness—could happen close together loads of times?"

"Yep," said Deer. "Not only that, but sometimes it's hard to remember the precise timing of changes in a child's

Andrew Wakefield (1957-) became famous for publishing research suggesting a link between the MMR vaccination, colon inflammation, and autism. Following his research, many parents refused to have their children vaccinated, even though other scientists and journalists showed flaws in Wakefield's work.

Wakefield was born in England as the son of two doctors. He attended medical school and studied for a few years in Canada. After returning to England, he taught at the Royal Free Hospital School of Medicine. There he began his research into a connection between the MMR vaccine, abdominal disease, and autism.

The controversy began in 1998 when Dr. Wakefield published his research in a prestigious British medical journal. He wrote about 12 children whose autism symptoms had started around the same time as their MMR vaccine. Other doctors could not replicate his findings. Journalists dug up information that he had been paid by lawyers representing parents with autistic children. These lawyers could make millions in lawsuits if Wakefield could "prove" that vaccines caused autism. Journalist Brian Deer found that Wakefield had filed for a patent on a new measles vaccine. Deer later showed that Wakefield had changed interviews with the parents and even changed test results to support his hypothesis.

As the controversy deepened, Wakefield was asked to leave the Royal Free Hospital. He moved to Austin, Texas. There, he and another opponent to the MMR vaccine set up their own clinic.

In 2010, the U.K. General Medical Council withdrew Wakefield's license to practice medicine. He quit the Texas clinic, but continued to live in the United States.

behavior or health. Parents want an answer to what caused this illness, and they want to believe in a charismatic doctor who says he has the answer and can help get them money for their child. So if Wakefield kept asking if those children's symptoms came on at just the right time, the parents eventually agreed."

"That's not right," Mae said. "That's not how scientists work. You're supposed to look at the evidence, not choose the evidence you like! I mean, of all the parents with autistic kids, he went out and *chose* the ones most likely to give him the story he wanted. That's a kind of cheating, isn't it?" She frowned and added, thinking of the GAS motto, "You're supposed to have scientific integrity."

"Scientific integrity... Yes, it must always be defended," Deer said, giving Mae a strange look.

"Through the centuries!" shouted Clinton, and Deer burst into happy laughter. He gave a slight bow. "So glad to help in training a new generation. So, children, what would be the proper way to look for an association between MMR and autism?"

Mae thought for a while. "Well, you couldn't just use parents who had already decided there was a link. You should look at all the kids you could find in some country or town or something who got the shots..."

"And all the kids who turned out autistic," Clinton half yelled.

"And then you'd see if… if there are more kids turning autistic right after the shots than other times, I guess," Mae said. "And if some kids never got the shot, you could see how many of them turned out to be autistic too."

"I think you get it," Deer said. "Now, even though Wakefield goes around the world giving talks about how evil the MMR vaccine is, he's never replicated his results— that is, tried the experiment again and had it come out the same way."

"That sounds bad," Clinton said.

"That *is* bad," Mr. Deer said, "but it gets worse. I found out that before he even did his study he filed for a patent on a new measles vaccine. If he could discredit the MMR vaccine, parents might use his vaccine instead. He would make loads of money."

"But why didn't someone stop him?" Clinton was outraged.

"Doctors have criticized his research and tried to tell the public. But maybe they're not as exciting speakers as Dr. Wakefield, because their message just doesn't get through. Wakefield knows how to get publicity. He even traveled to America to appear on TV news saying there was an epidemic of autism. People started to believe everything he said without checking out the science. Grieving parents jumped on his side and told stories of their children who were autistic."

"But did Wakefield ever prove that it was because of the MMR?" Clinton asked.

Brian Deer shook his head. "Other scientists found no connection between MMR and autism in the thousands of cases that they looked at," Mr. Deer said. "It got so uncomfortable here in England for Dr. Wakefield that he moved to Austin, Texas to get away. He started his own center for children with autism."

"He's in the United States?" Clinton asked.

"That's the last I heard," Mr. Deer said.

"Thanks, Mr. Deer," Mae said, glancing at the X-PA. "We have to go now."

Brian Deer closed his hand on something under the neck of his shirt—something that seemed to have the shape and hardness of a metal disk—just like the GAS medals Mae and Clinton wore. He gave the two kids a wink and a salute.

As they walked down the steps of the Times building, Mae said, "Wakefield is doing this all wrong. Think about Dr. Salk. He had the testing done on his vaccine, and he made sure he wouldn't know ahead of time what the results would show. He even refused to make money on his vaccine. That's real scientific integrity."

"I agree," Clinton said. "Nothing sounds right about this Wakefield guy. He went into his research hoping to make money on a vaccine. He rigged his research to come out a certain way. He hasn't repeated his results and nobody else can either. Where are we going next?"

Mae held out the X-PA. This time it showed just a date, May 2010, and a place, London. "Looks like this story isn't over yet."

Mae looped the Assistant and they landed at the back of another building.

"Now we're getting close to our time," Clinton said. He stopped a young woman with long straight red hair who seemed to be waiting outside the building and said, "Do you know what's going on in there?"

"It's the final meeting of the General Medical Council. They've been deliberating for months. I think they're going to stop that fraud Wakefield from practicing medicine. It's about time."

"Do you know Dr. Wakefield?" Mae asked.

"No. I'm just a medical student—name's Maureen, by the way—but he's giving all doctors a bad name with his tricks and lies."

Maureen intercepted a man in a pinstriped suit as he walked down the steps and asked, "Is there a verdict?"

"It's against Wakefield," the man said. Mae and Clinton crowded close to listen.

"They said he was dishonest and misleading. They stated that the case wasn't about whether the MMR vaccination causes autism. But they said that Wakefield acted in an unethical manner. He did unnecessary tests on troubled kids without getting proper permissions, and he didn't reveal conflicts of interest—how he was planning to make big money off a new vaccine. I think they'll take his license for this."

"Will parents listen to doctors now and resume getting their children vaccinated?" Maureen asked.

"I don't know," the man said. "I hope so."

Maureen turned to Mae and Clinton. "Britain used to vaccinate over 95% of its children, but with the vaccine scare, that fell to below 80%. In some parts of London, fewer than half of all children receive their MMR vaccines. We've been seeing outbreaks of measles we never thought we'd see again. Now I hope they can be prevented."

Clinton said, "But measles isn't really that bad a disease, is it?"

The student shook her head. "That's true for most people, as long as they're well-nourished and don't have

111

other illnesses already. In Britain and the US, only about three people die for every one thousand who get infected. But in Africa and India, where people are poor and there are fewer vaccines, about a hundred thousand kids a year die from measles. Another thousand kids are left blind."

Mae gulped, picturing a crying toddler unable to see its mother. "Those poor kids."

Just then a crowd of adults surged toward them. One middle-aged woman with a red face raised her fist and shouted, "Shame! The GMC is in the grip of the drug companies."

Another woman shouted, "This judgment is a travesty! They're hounding the only man with courage to tell the truth!"

The red-haired medical student sighed and said, "Do you think I should try to talk to them?"

A man yelled, "Dr. Wakefield is the only one who stands with parents of autistic children!" He shook his sign and advanced. "Down with the corporate flunkies seeking to hound him out of practice!"

"Uh," said Clinton. "Sorry to abandon you. We have to go. Thanks a lot, and good luck."

Mae shook hands with the student, and she and Clinton hurried around the corner.

"Just one last visit," Clinton said. "Looks like Mexico, 2010, but I don't see a person's name. You want to be the one to take us there?"

"I don't like the way this thing is acting up," Mae said, but she gritted her teeth and swung the X-PA in a loop all the same.

Chapter 9

Pandemic Flu

Veracruz, 2009

Mae and Clinton landed between a bush and the window of a small building. Cars honked and brakes groaned nearby. When they peeked out from their spot, Mae's hand went to her face. Nearly everybody walking past wore a white surgical mask, as if all the workers in a hospital had decided to go for a stroll. But some of the people wearing masks were children younger than Mae and Clinton.

Mae checked the X-PA and read aloud, "Rosa Hernandez, doctor at clinic, Veracruz, Mexico, 2009."

"You'd better switch the translator to Spanish, Mae," Clinton said. "Then we can look for the clinic."

"Maybe we should put on the masks that Selectra gave us," Mae said. "Do you still have yours?"

"Good idea." Clinton pulled the transparent, filmy mask out of his pocket and fit it over his face. Mae did the same. Mae pressed the translation button, and she and Clinton walked around the corner of the building. A long line of people, some of them sweating, others coughing, stood waiting outside a door marked *Clínica*.

"Oh," said Clinton. "I guess we found the clinic." He started to push toward the front of the line, but Mae grabbed hold of his arm.

"What?" demanded Clinton. "If we just wait in line like everyone else, the site energy will run out way before we get to the front."

People around them shuffled and muttered.

"Maybe," Mae said. "But these people are sick. They don't want to see us cutting the line."

Clinton thought for a moment. "Okay." He led the way back around the building and behind the bush. "I guess that's why the Assistant brought us right here. The window's open. You first?"

Still uncertain, Mae stepped into the stirrup Clinton made with his hands and crawled through the window. Then she reached back to help him, but he brushed her off. "No need. I'm an athlete, remember?" He hoisted himself, ducked through the window, and landed in a tumble on

the floor. Glassware rattled on the shelves around him, but luckily nothing fell.

Clinton stood and brushed off his jeans. "Looks like a storeroom. Hey, check out these big refrigerators."

Just then, the door to the storeroom opened, and a pretty Latina woman with red lipstick and a white coat entered the room. On seeing them, she gasped and clapped a hand to her mouth.

Clinton extended his hand. "Hello, I'm Clinton Chang. And you must be Dr. Rosa Hernandez."

"What are you two children doing here?" the doctor said. "And why aren't you wearing masks?"

"We have masks…." Clinton began. Then he added, "We're visiting students, and we really need to learn about this disease. Can you spare us just a minute?"

Dr. Hernandez looked at him with her lips pressed together. Then she sighed, reached for a shelf, and handed them two masks. "Put these on. You're from the United States, aren't you? Your Spanish is very good. Quick, what do you need to know? Are you sick?"

"No, we're not sick," Mae said. "But what's going on? Are all those people waiting outside the door sick?"

"They hear swine flu and they panic. Even those who aren't really sick begin to feel a headache or some muscle pains."

"Swine flu!" Clinton said. "Pigs get the flu?"

"Yes, pig and birds, and sometimes that swine or bird flu virus mutates, or changes, enough that it can infect humans. The scientific name for this particular strain in Mexico now is influenza A-H1N1, named for the type of flu markers on the virus surface," Dr. Hernandez said. "People are afraid, because the awful influenza in 1918 was also H1N1. That flu killed 50 to 100 million people all over the world."

"Flu killed that many people?" Clinton gulped. "I mean, I guess we heard that before, but to think that kind of flu can come back, that's really scary."

Mae's stomach tightened at the thought of the little children snuggling in their parents' arms at the door of the clinic. She adjusted her glasses and asked, "Is it really the same flu now?"

"We're not sure, but we're doing everything we can to keep people from getting the disease. Schools are closed, and most other meeting places are too. Now we're vaccinating everyone we can reach and hoping for the best. Of course, some people are more afraid of the vaccine than the disease."

"What are they worried about?" Mae asked. "Don't they realize a shot is better than getting a terrible disease like that one you told us about?"

"We don't know for sure if this is the same flu or as strong as that one in 1918. In 1976 in the US, a few soldiers died from H1N1 flu. It scared everyone, so President Gerald Ford asked all Americans to be vaccinated. The vaccination program started, but then a controversy arose about the vaccine."

"Did people get flu from it?" Clinton asked.

"No, but a few, very few, people who received the flu shot got a condition called Guillain-Barré syndrome. It's a form of paralysis."

Mae shuddered. "Do the people have to be in iron lungs?"

"No, that's from the days of polio epidemics. Sometimes people with Guillan-Barré have to stay in the hospital on respirators to help them breathe for weeks or even months, but in time, the paralysis goes away."

Mae said, "So the swine flu vaccine caused this Guillain-Barré syndrome?'

Dr. Hernandez shrugged. "Even today we are not certain. One study showed Guillain-Barré happened in one out of every one million vaccinated people, but other studies have shown an even lower rate. The thing is that Guillain-Barré happens sometimes anyway, without a person being vaccinated. Still, it scares people."

"It scares me," Clinton said.

"I know what you mean," Dr. Hernandez said. "When that epidemic started, my family was living in the United States. I was just a small girl, but my aunt contracted Guillain-Barré. She was paralyzed for a while. I remember visiting her in the hospital with that big respirator whooshing the air in and out of her lungs. That experience made me want to be a doctor. So now here I am, treating people with the flu and vaccinating others so they won't get it."

"How can you stand to give people vaccines if it made your aunt be paralyzed?" Clinton asked.

"You have to remember that the chance of paralysis is very small. With flu, the chance of other complications, like pneumonia, is large. I'd rather vaccinate as many people as possible rather than have to treat so much pneumonia and see people die from the flu. Already, here in Mexico, more than fifty people have died."

"But still, being paralyzed," Clinton said.

"It's a hard choice, I agree," Dr. Hernandez said. Then she went on, "You're here for school, are you? How will you get home to the U.S. if they stop the planes from flying into Veracruz?"

"They might stop the planes?" Mae said.

"It's been talked about. Governments are trying to stop this from becoming a pandemic."

"Is a pandemic worse than an epidemic?" Mae asked.

"Not always," Dr. Hernandez answered. "A pandemic just means that there are disease cases on more than one continent. The disease is seen in different places around the world and that usually happens from air travel. So watch that you don't get stranded here. I'd better get back to work. I have so many patients to see. I only came in here to get another case of vaccine from the refrigerator."

"You keep it in the refrigerator?" Clinton asked.

"Yes. Vaccines have to be kept within a very narrow, cold temperature band right up until the time we inject them. Otherwise the proteins in them warm up, unfold, and become inactive. That's one of the reasons vaccinating people in rural areas or poor countries where there's not good refrigeration can be difficult." Dr. Hernandez opened the large refrigerator behind Mae and lifted out a small tray of glass vials. "Luckily, here, we're very well supplied. Now, you'll show yourselves out, will you? And be careful."

"Thank you so much for explaining it to us," Mae said.

When Dr. Hernandez closed the door behind her, Mae looked at Clinton. "I'm wiped out. How about you?"

"Me too," Clinton said. "I think my brain is tired from thinking. This vaccine stuff is pretty crazy." He scratched his nose. "I sure don't want to get polio, and the flu can be pretty bad. Mumps and chickenpox are awful. But a vaccine can paralyze you. I wish I knew what's right."

"Maybe one in a million times," Mae reminded him. "Besides, my mom says that there are risks in our lives all the time."

"But not to get hurt like this Guillain-Barré thing," Clinton said. "I mean, not being able to move!"

"Almost every day at home, you get in the car and go somewhere. That's a risk," Mae said.

"No big deal," Clinton said.

"Tell that to Madison Spencer. Her family was in a car accident and she broke her leg. Her mom almost died," Mae said.

Clinton looked at her with surprise. "I guess you're right. I never thought of a car ride being that dangerous."

"Better check the **Site Energy** bar," Mae said. "How are we doing?"

"Lowish. We'd better go. Good thing we don't have to get on a plane."

"We're going home, I hope," Mae said.

"Yeah," Clinton said slowly. "Maybe we know as much as we need. I was kind of hoping we'd get an absolute answer, but I guess we're not going to. It might be time to go home and see what's happening with the UFV."

"Homeward bound," Mae said, and as Clinton enclosed the loop, she felt the familiar tug, and darkness closed around her.

Chapter 10
The Pharmacist's Assistant

They landed softly on the darkened grass in front of Mae's apartment complex. "I still can't decide," Clinton said. "Flu can be really bad, but what about those side effects?"

"I don't know," said Mae. "What side effects, really?"

"Well, autism for one. I mean, I know Dr. Wakefield had no real proof, but…"

"See, that's the problem with scientific fraud," Mae said. "You know there's no evidence, you know Wakefield changed the data for his own profit, and you know from Brian Deer that studies have shown no connection between autism and vaccines. And still that idea somehow sticks in your mind. It's in my mind too, I admit it. But I think we have to go with the evidence."

"But then there's that Guillain-Barré thing. What about the risk of getting paralyzed?"

"That's terrible, but Dr. Hernandez said it was a one in a million chance. One in a million, Clinton! That's a pretty small chance. I bet it's a lot less than the chance of dying from the flu."

Clinton chewed on his lip and twisted around, digging his toe into the grass. "I don't know. It's hard to decide," he said. "I'm too tired to think, so I guess I'll go home and see you tomorrow."

"Call me in the morning," Mae said.

As Clinton walked off through the darkness, Mae entered the building. When she reached her apartment, she opened the door and crept to her mother's room. She heard her mother inside, still packing, so Mae tiptoed to her room and got ready for bed. But once she was in bed, she couldn't sleep. So many images of what they had seen and heard flew through her head—people in iron lungs or on crutches, people with smallpox, others with Guillain-Barré, some in the hospital with pneumonia from flu complications. The thought of all that illness was scary. Then she remembered that so-called scientist, Andrew Wakefield. He was a fraud, and Mae hated the idea of him being even thought of as a scientist. She remembered Brian Deer's special salute to them, and she smiled to think of him as a fellow GAS member out there, working as a journalist and fighting to preserve scientific integrity. Finally, she fell asleep.

The next morning, Mae said goodbye as her mother headed out for her meeting at the state capital. "Be careful, Mom," Mae said. "Stay away from protestors."

"Be good for Mrs. Peach," her mother answered.

Because it was a Saturday, Mae grabbed a bowl of cereal and glass of milk and settled down in front of the TV. People carrying signs still mobbed the county health offices. It looked like the crowd of protestors had doubled since the night before. Then the image switched to a man sitting in the news studio. The anchorperson introduced him as Dr. Wellman and said that he was one of the researchers who had developed the Universal Flu Vaccine. Mae turned up the sound to hear what he said. She wished Clinton were here, too. Just then her doorbell rang.

"Clinton, come in and hear this," Mae said. She picked up the remote and ran the DVR back to play the start of Dr. Wellman's comments.

"The vaccine we have made protects against every kind of flu. It has been tested with excellent results. It provides immunity from the flu, and it has not caused side effects other than an occasional mild fever and soreness at the injection site."

"Why do we have to get flu shots every year?" the anchor asked.

"Yeah, that's what I want to know," Clinton said.

Dr. Wellman picked up a white board and drew on it. He said, "Influenza is a virus, much smaller than a bacterium. The flu virus contains genetic material in a round protein envelope, like a tiny sphere."

He drew round shapes on the board. "The sphere has strings attached to it which are molecules called glycoproteins. That means they are part protein and part sugar. The kinds of glycoproteins determine what type of flu it is."

"How many kinds of flu are there?" the anchor asked.

"There are three main types, A, B, and C. C is a mild flu, more like a cold. B spreads among humans, but doesn't cause widespread flu pandemics. A is the one most likely to cause a pandemic, and it has subsets within it. The H and N markers, such as when we say H1N1 or H2N5, refer to the kinds of glycoproteins sticking out from the surface. The immune system, specifically B-lymphocytes, recognizes the flu virus by the H and N markers, and then the lymphocytes and other white blood cells will kill any of that virus they see. "

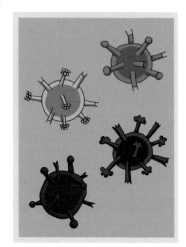

"And why do we get the shots every year?" the anchor asked again.

"The flu virus mutates, which means it changes frequently, almost as if it's wearing a disguise. It changes its H and N markers. So every year, we observe early signs to predict what H and N strains will predominate for that year. Then we make the vaccine. The vaccine, which is a form of killed influenza virus, stimulates the body's immune system to respond and build antibodies against the glycoproteins in that year's flu. After that, if live virus infects the person, the antibodies remember and attack the virus before it can get enough of a foothold to make the person sick."

"But many people claim that they get the flu after they've had the shot. Why is that?"

"Some people get colds and think it's the flu. Some were already infected with the flu before they got the shot, and the vaccine doesn't have time to prevent the symptoms.

And then, of course, the vaccine is not always effective in every person. Some people will still get the flu. And sometimes, worst of all, the virus tricks us. We guess wrong about what strain will spread that year. But until now, these seasonal vaccines were the best we had."

"How does this relate to the UFV?"

"Scientists have been working on a Universal Flu Vaccine for years. If a vaccine could be made that produced the right antibody response for all kinds of flu, yearly injections would no longer be necessary. Now we've succeeded. Our new UFV targets the part of the influenza virus that doesn't change, so it will work against all kinds of flu."

Clinton said, "Hey, Mae! You were right. That's how they do it!"

"Lots of people are worried about the safety of this new vaccine," the anchor said.

"We've followed every governmental procedure and even done more testing than is required. Actually, we're seeing fewer problems with this vaccine than we have with those that have been used for years. Side effects are infrequent and mild," Dr. Wellman said. "It would be a shame if people let rumors scare them away from the vaccine. Serious complications from the flu are much more likely than problems with the vaccine."

"Do you think that's right?" Clinton asked Mae. "I mean, they may test the vaccine on hundreds or thousands of people, but some side effects are one in a million."

"I think it's better to get the vaccine," Mae said. "Partly I'm going on doctors and scientists and my mom saying it's all right, but a big part is because of what we've seen on this mission. Just think of all the diseases that we don't have to worry about because of vaccines."

"I'm starting to agree with you," Clinton said slowly. "In fact, I'm starting to worry the other way. I talked to my parents about how my sister Chelsea might have an allergy to eggs. Dr. Hilleman said someone who does shouldn't get the vaccine. Now I'm worried about her health if she doesn't get the shot. How crazy is that?"

"I don't think it's crazy," Mae said. "This whole vaccine thing is complicated." She thought for a minute. "You know, the pharmacy where Mom and I go is starting to give the vaccine today. I wonder if they'll have any customers."

"We could go see," Clinton said. "I rode my bike."

After Mae told Mrs. Peach she was going for a bike ride, she met Clinton outside. They pedaled down the street to the main road and then a few blocks away to the Mitchell Pharmacy. They left their bikes in a rack behind the store.

A few people wandered out of the store rubbing their arms, but when Clinton and Mae entered, the checkout area didn't seem any busier than usual. Mae led Clinton to the back corner where the pharmacy was.

"We usually get our flu shots back here," she said.

A sign on the counter read, "Flu shots closed for lunch. Please return after two."

"Hmm," said Mae. "Looks like we just missed the action. Maybe we can talk to the pharmacist." She leaned on the counter and peered past the shelves. Behind them, the broad back of a man partially blocked her view of a refrigerator inside the pharmacy area. The young man turned around and said, "The pharmacy is closed right now. The pharmacist is taking a short break. Come back after two."

Mae couldn't say a word. Now she knew where she had seen the man she'd recognized at the anti-vaccine rally. His nametag said "Carl." He kept looking at her, and Mae realized that he was holding several vaccine vials in a box. He set them down on a table next to some other boxes full of vials. Glaring at Mae, he said, "Did you understand me, kid? Run along."

Mae finally found her voice and said, "Okay, we'll come back later."

She turned away from the counter and led the way to the store's candy section, where she ran her hands over the packages of different candy bars. Clinton followed. "What's going on, Mae?" Clinton said. "Why didn't you ask him how the vaccinations are going?"

"I knew I recognized him from somewhere," Mae said in a whisper. "I saw him on TV. He was at one of the protests, waving a sign. I think it was the one that said AUTISM with a big red X over it."

"And he works in a pharmacy? Wow, that's crazy," Clinton said.

Mae walked to the front of the store. Something hung in the back of her mind, bothering her, but she wasn't sure what.

Clinton bought two smoothies at the counter, and they went outside and sat on the curb. Without a word, Clinton, who seemed to understand that Mae was thinking hard, passed her the smoothie. When she felt the cold of the drink cup in her hand, Mae's mind clicked.

"Clinton, I think something is wrong. Those vials that we saw in the boxes. If those are flu vaccine, they have to be cold, and he was taking them out of the refrigerator."

"Why would he do that?" Clinton asked. Then his eyes opened wide. "Do you think he's trying to ruin the vaccine? Maybe he wants to make it no good so people won't get it?"

"Maybe that's what he wants," Mae agreed slowly.

Clinton stood up and said, "We shouldn't jump to conclusions. Maybe he was just checking them for a moment."

Mae frowned. "Maybe. Being out of the refrigerator for just a couple of minutes wouldn't hurt the vaccine."

"On the other hand," Clinton said, "if the vials are still out by the time we finish our smoothies, that could mean something."

They slurped down the smoothies and threw away the cups. Then they entered the store again and crept up to the prescription counter. They crouched under the window and rose slowly, barely peeking over the edge. For just a minute, they caught a glimpse of Carl. He held in his hand a large syringe full of a pale liquid, and as they watched, he injected the liquid into one of the vaccine vials. As he drew the needle from the vial, he looked up at the wall in front of him. Mae was shocked to see his face in a mirror on the wall. Clearly, he saw them also, and his face twisted into a snarl of anger.

"Come on! Let's go." Mae yanked on Clinton's sleeve.

"Hey, you kids!" Carl yelled, whirling to face them. "I told you to get out of here." He held the syringe behind his back.

Mae spun away from the window. She and Clinton flew back through the store and out the door.

"Whew, that was close," Clinton said. "But what was he doing?"

"I don't know," Mae said. "Do you think he was putting something in the vials or taking it out?"

"Not sure," Clinton said. "But we better get out of here before he comes after us with that syringe."

They walked quickly to the back of the store where they had left their bikes. As they rounded the corner, Clinton stuck out his hand and grabbed Mae's arm.

"Wait," he said. "Someone's back there. I think it's the pharmacy guy."

As they peeked around the corner, a car pulled out of the alley on the far side of the pharmacy and stopped just at the back door. Mae and Clinton crouched behind some trashcans and watched as the driver's window rolled down. Carl bent to talk to the person inside. Mae saw a woman's head in the car, but she couldn't make out the woman's face.

"I'm going closer to see what's going on," Clinton said.

"No, Clinton," Mae started, but he was already sneaking forward to hide behind a dumpster. Mae sighed and crept after him.

"…too dangerous," she heard Carl say. "Going to take more money. If they figure out all the bad vaccine came from this one store, I'll be in big trouble. And there were two kids snooping around."

Then the woman in the car spoke and Clinton turned to look at Mae with raised eyebrows. Mae nodded. She recognized that piercing voice—Candidate Margo Smearon.

"Who were the kids?" she asked. "I'm sure they won't figure anything out."

"Don't be so sure," Carl said. "The girl's mother of is a customer of ours, and I know she works for the research firm that tested the vaccine. That kid might know a lot, and I think she saw me with the syringe."

"Can you find her? Do you know where they live?"

Mae's throat tightened, and her stomach started to hurt. Clinton's mouth hung open.

"I can find out," Carl said. "It'll be in the pharmacy records. But this will definitely take more money."

"You'll get your money," Smearon said. "Campaign donations will come pouring in after this. I've got to go. Do what you were told and call my cell with that address. I'll handle the kids."

Chapter 11

The Chase is On

Mae felt as if her muscles had frozen. Clinton tugged on her sleeve, but all she could think about was that someone wanted to hurt her or her mother, and they knew her address.

"Come on, Mae," Clinton urged.

Finally, once Margo Smearon drove away and Carl disappeared back into the pharmacy, Mae unfroze, and she and Clinton hurried back to their bikes. They pedaled away as fast as they could, and Mae kept her head low because she had the creepy sensation that someone was following them.

When they were about three blocks from the pharmacy, they paused at a red light. Clinton turned to Mae and

said, "Where can we go? We've got to tell someone before anybody gets that messed-up vaccine."

"I don't know. Can't go back to my house because that man knows…." Mae gulped and couldn't finish.

"Yeah, I know, and my parents will think we're making it up," Clinton said.

Mae thought hard. She said, "If I call my mom, maybe she'll be out of her meeting and I can make her listen to us. But I can't even think out here on the street. What if Carl drives by and sees us?"

"I know where we can hide," Clinton said. "I have a place at school."

They sped away down the street. When they reached the school grounds, Clinton rode to the side of the gym building where some hydrangeas grew. He pushed his bike through the bushes and then turned to help Mae. "Sometimes I come here just to think," he said. "No one ever sees me."

Mae steered her bike through the bushes to a space like a little cave between the bushes and the gym wall. She leaned against the wall to catch her breath.

"This is awful, Clinton. That man Carl wants to hurt us because of what we saw, but what he's doing is going to hurt a lot of people. Why would he ruin that vaccine? What if that was poison he was putting in there? Or…"

"Call your mom, Mae. She might be able to get that vaccine checked. At least she can call the police. They probably wouldn't believe two kids."

Mae pulled her cell phone out of her pocket with shaking hands. It was the wrong pocket. What she pulled out was the X-PA. She handed it to Clinton and dug in the other pocket for her phone.

Clinton gazed at the X-PA. "Do you think Selectra knew all this was going to happen?"

"I don't know. I hadn't thought about it," Mae said as she pushed the button to call her mom.

The phone rang four times and then her mother's recorded voice came on. Mae sighed. She would have to leave a message.

She began in a shaky voice, "Mom, please call me...."

Mid-message, her mother picked up. "Mae, is that you? Are you all right? Where are you?" Her mother sounded a little shaky, too.

"Mom, I'm all right, but something happened and we have to tell you."

Before Mae could say more, her mother interrupted. "Mrs. Peach just called and said that someone painted a threat on our apartment door. I was so worried. Where are you?"

"I'm with Clinton, and we're hiding at the school. Listen, Mom." She went on to tell her mother what they had seen at the pharmacy.

She finished, "I don't know why Carl would do that, but we saw him on the TV, too. He was at one of the anti-vaccine protests."

"You say he was putting something in the vaccine vials." Her mother couldn't seem to take in what Mae was saying.

"Yes. And then we heard him talking to Margo Smearon, and he said he knew me and where I lived. She told him to do his job and she'd take care of us kids."

"Oh, Mae! This is terrible! I wish I were home."

After a moment, her mother spoke in a calmer voice. "Here's what I want you to do. There's a police station about four blocks from the school. You and Clinton start riding your bikes north on Hamilton right now. Keep your phone on so I can hear you. When you get to the station, I'll call and tell them what's going on. Start right now."

"Mom wants us to go to the police station, Clinton."

"Good idea," Clinton said.

They wheeled back onto the street and rode in the direction of the police station. Mae held her phone in one hand against the handle bar. She could barely pedal because all her muscles seemed to be tensing up. She heard Clinton gasp, and he pulled up right next to her.

"Look down or something, Mae," he said in a low voice. "That's the same kind of car that Smearon had."

Mae's stomach lurched. The car slowed down as it passed them, but then it sped away.

As they pulled into the parking lot of the police station, Mae heard her mother yelling on the phone.

"Mae, are you all right? Are you there yet?"

"We're here, Mom."

"I'm calling them now. Just go inside and wait."

Mae and Clinton walked in the door of the station. The female officer at the desk said, "What can I do for you kids?"

"Her mom is calling about a crime, I think it's a crime, that we saw," Clinton said.

"A crime, huh?" the officer said. "Why don't you just sit down over there and we'll see what this is about."

Mae and Clinton sat on hard plastic chairs for what seemed like a month. Finally, another police officer came through a door and walked over to them.

"I'm Officer Legg," he said. "And you are Mae Harris and Clinton Chang?"

"Yes, sir," Clinton said. Mae had never heard him be so polite.

"Come with me, and we'll get your statement about what you saw."

As they walked through door away from the front desk, Mae said, "Isn't anyone checking it out? They could be giving someone poisoned vaccine right this minute."

"We have officers at the pharmacy now. They'll confiscate all the vaccine to ensure the safety of the public until we can test it."

"But even if it doesn't have poison, Carl left it out," Mae said. "It's supposed to be refrigerated, but he left it sitting on the table."

"And we saw Margo Smearon saying she would pay him money to mess it up," Clinton said.

"It's all being investigated," Officer Legg said. "I just need to hear your story from the beginning." He settled down behind a desk, and Mae and Clinton sat in chairs across from him.

"Can we have something to drink before we start?" Clinton asked.

Mae looked at him in surprise. They had just drunk big smoothies outside the pharmacy.

"Coke? Water?" asked Officer Legg.

"Water would be great," Clinton said.

Mae just nodded her head. Officer Legg disappeared into the hall. Clinton leaned close and spoke in Mae's ear as other police officers wrote at their desks or talked on phones.

"Mae, we can't tell them anything about Selectra or the X-PA or anything," Clinton said.

"You asked for a drink just to tell me that? I can figure that out for myself."

"Here he comes," Clinton said.

Officer Legg sat down behind the desk and handed them paper cups full of water.

"We need you to tell us what you saw. With your permission, we'll record your evidence. Your mother has given us permission, Mae. We are trying to reach your parents, Clinton. I'm sure we'll locate them soon, but until then, why don't you just let Mae do the talking."

Clinton groaned and said, "But we're telling the truth, Officer Legg."

"I must have parental permission to question juveniles, even if they're not charged with anything," Officer Legg explained. "So, we'll start with you, Mae. What happened at the pharmacy?"

Mae told her story again, and then she repeated most of it as Officer Legg asked the same questions over and over in slightly different ways. When she was telling it for about the third time, Clinton's parents arrived. His father had grey hair and glasses, and his mother wore a flowered dress and a string of pearls that she kept rotating with nervous fingers. Officer Legg pulled up two more chairs and began to go over with Clinton the same questions he had asked Mae.

When Clinton told about Margo Smearon's threats, his mother gasped and reached over from her chair to clasp Clinton against her. Mae's eyes teared up, and she wished her own mom were with them. Almost before that thought had sunk through her tired mind, she heard her mother say her name.

"Mae, I got here as fast as I could. Are you sure you're all right?"

Mae threw her arms around her mother and said, "I'm fine, Mom. But what about all those vaccines?"

"Your daughter is really worried about those vaccines. She even knew they might be destroyed by not being in the refrigerator," Officer Legg said.

"How did you know that, Mae?" Mom sounded surprised.

Glancing at Clinton, Mae said, "Well, I do listen to you sometimes. Once I heard you talking about it from work."

Clinton gave her a thumbs-up with his hand in his lap so no one else could see.

Officer Legg continued to ask Clinton about the incident for a while longer. Just when Mae didn't think she could stand to hear anything more about it, the phone rang and Officer Legg answered.

When he hung up, he said, "They're bringing Carl Batty in now. He's already trying to confess. I think we can let you kids go home and relax, and we'll take it from here."

As they stood up, he reached out to shake hands with Clinton and Mae. "You kids did a brave thing, and lots of people will have reason to thank you."

Mae's mom squeezed Mae's bike into the car and headed home. Mae's head drooped with fatigue, and as soon as they reached the apartment, she stumbled into her room and fell onto her bed to sleep.

Mae woke an hour or two later to the sound of her mother's voice rising and falling in the other room. The phone clicked off, and then Mae's mother burst into the room and grabbed Mae into a tight hug.

"Mae, I'm sure you and Clinton have saved people's lives," she said. "Carl confessed that Margo Smearon paid him $50,000 to ruin the vaccine by leaving some of it out of the refrigerator. That meant that people would still get the flu and would think that Candidate Smearon was right to fight against the vaccine. But Smearon was worried that those results would be too slow and uncertain, so she did an even worse thing. She gave Carl a liquid to put in the vials. She told him that it was water that would dilute the vaccine to make it weaker."

Mom took a big breath, and Mae waited.

"But really it was worse, much worse. The liquid had peanut oil in it. If someone who was allergic to peanuts got that dose…" Mom's voice trailed off.

"You mean, they could die?" Mae couldn't believe her ears. "Why would she do that?"

"If news stories reported people becoming sick, or dying, from the vaccine, or lots of people still getting the flu in spite of the vaccine, then Smearon's crusade against the vaccine would make her seem wise and heroic. A vaccine disaster would make it easy for Smearon to be elected to the Senate. It's hard to believe, but apparently she was willing to put people's lives at risk for her own ambition."

Mom continued, "Officer Legg said Carl swears he didn't know it was peanut oil. Carl just wanted to keep people from getting the vaccine. He has a son with autism, and he believes a vaccine caused it. He just wanted to do something to stop all vaccines."

Mom hugged Mae again and said, "I am so proud of you, Mae. You saw something wrong and you acted on it. You and Clinton are real heroes."

"We were just paying attention, Mom. No big deal," Mae said. She thought of Brian Deer's salute, smiled, and added, "Besides, throughout the centuries, there always has to be someone willing to defend scientific integrity. I guess it was just our turn."

Chapter 12

Cheerio and Frosted Flakes

The following morning, Mae sat on her bed, too rest-less to do anything. She had tried to read, checked e-mail, played a computer game, and done a few problems of math homework, but nothing held her attention. She opened a drawer and reached under her socks to pull out a medal hanging on a string of ribbon. One side of the medal read, "Mae Jemison Harris, Trainee." Printed around the edge were the words, "Galactic Academy of Science" and on the other side, "Defending scientific integrity through the cen-turies."

Mae turned the medal over in her hand, thinking about the vaccine mission, when she heard a knock at the door. She stuck the medal back in the drawer as Clinton walked in. He grinned when he saw what she was putting away.

"I've been looking at mine, too," he said. "Do you think we'll get to go on any more GAS missions? Or see Selectra again?"

Just then, with a small thump, Selectra plopped into view next to Mae, resplendent in pink and green. She held out her hand for the X-PA, and Mae handed it over even as Selectra began to speak.

"Greetings, dudes from the past," Selectra said. "Your grade for this mission: A-1 zwiffy. Tough, wasn't it? But you did it."

"Did you know we were going to get threatened?" Clinton asked.

"I wasn't sure exactly what you two would do, but we knew there was a threat against the vaccine. Now it's safe, thanks to the two of you. Roasting!" Selectra said.

Clinton said, "My family got our vaccine shots this morning, all except for Chelsea." He sat on the bed. "The nurse said if there was a question of egg allergy she'd be better off without the vaccine. So then I asked her if enough people were going to get the vaccine to provide people like my sister with herd immunity." He laughed. "Boy, was she surprised by that question. She gave me this look like I must be really smart."

Mae said, "You are smart. But what did she say about the herd immunity?"

"She said if enough people get the vaccine, like ninety percent or something, then people like Chelsea who can't get it will still be protected, because the virus won't be able to spread." He scratched his head. "I wonder if this means I have to start speaking out in favor of the vaccine."

"I'll help you," offered Mae. "But I'll try not to promise any miracles."

Selectra said, "Listen to you two bubble along. To think you were so fungal you'd hardly speak to each other two days ago. I guess it just goes to show that with a little respect and open-mindedness, two people can look at evidence together and resolve an argument."

Clinton said, "Oh, hey, that reminds me why I came over. All the Sunday shows are going to show the news of Margo Smearon's nasty plot and wonderful arrest. Want to stay and watch with us, Selectra?"

Selectra waved her hand. "I prefer not. It's painful for a dudette from the future like me to watch your antiquated technology. Besides," she said with a frown, "I need to activate some more recruits, fast. Things are getting grooby at home. You didn't notice any malfunction of the X-PA, did you?" She turned the device over in her hand and studied it. "There have been rumors of someone trying to hack our whole system. Well, cheerio and frosted flakes!"

"Well, we did have some trouble..." Mae began, but Selectra was gone. Sighing, Mae pulled up a news site on her computer, and she and Clinton watched a video of Margo Smearon's arrest. The Senate candidate thrashed and yelled about her innocence, but the reporter detailed the story of her plan to have peanut oil put in the vaccine and use that tragedy to propel herself to the Senate. He said, "The amazing thing is that it was two kids—their parents prefer to keep them anonymous, and the police and journalists respect that request—whose alertness and bravery alerted the authorities to this vicious plot."

"We did it," Clinton said.

"It's a great feeling, isn't it?" Mae agreed. "Do you think vaccines are safe now, Clinton?"

Before Clinton could answer, Mae's mom stuck her head in the bedroom door. "Mae, it's time for us to go to the pharmacy for our UFV. Are you ready?"

"Ready, Mom," Mae said. "See you in school, Clinton. " She raised an arm and marched out the bedroom door, chanting, "Onward, for the integrity of science!"

ABOUT THE AUTHOR

Pendred Noyce is a physician, educator, mother of five, and children's author. She is a trustee of the Noyce Foundation, which supports efforts to improve K-12 math and science learning. Penny is also the author of the award-winning Lexicon Adventure series published by Scarletta Press.

Roberta Baxter is a children's author with a degree in chemistry. Her favorite topics are history and science, which she gets to combine in writing for the Galactic Academy of Science series. She has written eleven books, including a number of biographies of notable scientists and inventors.

COMING SOON

The Harrowing Case of the Hackensack Hacker

(Galactic Academy of Science Series)
Roberta Baxter/Barnas G. Monteith

The new tablet computer Anita and Benson bought for the engineering fair crashes whenever a creepy face flashes on the screen. Then Quarkum Phonon, while briefing them on a new mission for the Galactic Academy of Science, fades away with a look of terror on his face. Now Anita and Benson must race against time to learn about computer hacking, expose the enemies of G.A.S., try to save Quarkum and foil the computer virus that threatens to destroy the future of earth.

Something Stinks

Gail E. Hedrick

Dead fish are washing ashore on the Higdon River, and seventh grader Emily Sanders decides to find out why. Mocked by fellow students and abandoned by her best friend, Emily investigates farms, a golf course, and local factories. Gradually she persuades friends to help her test the waters. Their investigations lead them into trouble with the law and confrontation with the town's most powerful citizen. Can a handful of determined seventh graders find out the true source of the stink in the Higdon River?

MORE SCIENCE FUN IS ON THE HORIZON AT

TUMBLEHOME
l e a r n i n g

For experiments and activities illustrating the science in this book, order the **Virus Wars Game** *and the* **Virus Vaccine Science Kit** *today!*

Whether you're interested in engineering, dinosaurs, space, biology, or other wonders of the universe, we have something for you. Check out our website for more Galactic Academy of Science books and other fun and inspiring THL offerings:

www.tumblehomelearning.com

G.A.S. SERIES

Clinton and Mae's Missions:
The Desperate Case of the Diamond Chip
The Vicious Case of the Viral Vaccine
AND COMING SOON
The Baffling Case of the Battered Brain

Anita and Benson's Missions:
The Furious Case of the Fraudulent Fossil
The Harrowing Case of the Hackensack Hacker
AND COMING SOON
The Curious Case of the Climate Caper

... and more G.A.S. adventures on the way!

JOIN TODAY!
THE GALACTIC ACADEMY OF SCIENCE
NEEDS YOU!

Buy more Galactic Academy of Science titles at Amazon.com, Tumblehomelearning.com and retail outlets throughout the world. Other titles include: "The Desperate Case of the Diamond Chip", "The Furious Case of the Fraudulent Fossil", "The Harrowing Case of the Hackensack Hacker" and more. There's a subject of scientific interest for everybody!

The Galactic Academy of Science (G.A.S.)
Defending the integrity of science through the ages